THE
TATAMI
TIME
MACHINE
BLUES

THE
TATAMI
TIME
MACHINE
BLUES

A NOVEL

Tomihiko Morimi

Translated from the Japanese by Emily Balistrieri

HARPERVIA

An Imprint of HarperCollinsPublishers

THE TATAMI TIME MACHINE BLUES. Copyright © 2020 by Tomihiko Morimi and Makoto Ueda; English translation copyright © 2023 by Emily Balistrieri. All rights reserved. Printed in the United Kingdom. No part of this book may be used or reproduced in any manner whatsoever without written permission except in the case of brief quotations embodied in critical articles and reviews. For information, address HarperCollins Publishers, 195 Broadway, New York, NY 10007.

HarperCollins books may be purchased for educational, business, or sales promotional use. For information, please email the Special Markets Department at SPsales@harpercollins.com.

Originally published as *Yojō-Han Time Machine Blues* in Japan in 2020 by KADOKAWA Corporation; English-language rights arranged with KADOKAWA Corporation, Tokyo, through Tuttle-Mori Agency, Inc.

First HarperVia hardcover published 2023

Library of Congress Cataloging-in-Publication Data is available upon request.

ISBN 978-0-06-315849-8

ScoutAutomatedPrintCode

23 24 25 26 CPI 10 9 8 7 6 5 4 3

Contents

ONE

August 12

'm going to say it up front: I've never had a meaningful summer.

Summer is commonly said to be a season for personal growth. Meet a boy after one summer, and you'll hardly recognize him! In order to attain that glorious moment when you show off the new and improved you to your classmates, a detailed plan, early nights and early mornings, tempering of the flesh, and academic devotion are essential.

But in my third year living at my lodgings, I was spurred by impatience.

During the Kyoto summer, my four-and-a-half-mat tatami room transformed into a fiery hell on par with the Taklamakan Desert. In this environment, so harsh it's doubtful life could even be supported, I proceeded steadily toward the collapse of my daily rhythm, my detailed plan turned into an armchair fantasy, and summer fatigue hastened my flesh's deterioration and my academic corruption. Under such circumstances, not even Buddha himself would be able to attain growth as a person. Ah, even if one's dreams are dashed, the four-and-a-half-mat tatami room remains.

I had already passed the halfway point of the study period

known as "college." And yet I hadn't spent a single meaningful summer. I hadn't built myself into a person who could be of use to society. If I didn't stop twiddling my thumbs, society would no doubt heartlessly slam its gate in my face. The breakthrough for revitalization was that civilized convenience: an air conditioner.

• • •

It was the afternoon of August 12.

In my student apartment, room 209, I sat face-to-face with a man.

My base of operations was a room at Shimogamo Yusuiso in Shimogamo Izumikawacho. When I first visited the place on the university co-op's introduction, I thought I must have wandered into the walled city of Kowloon. The three-story wooden structure caused all those who saw it anxiety; it seemed ready to collapse at any moment. Its dilapidation was practically Important Cultural Property–level. Certainly no one would miss it if it burned down.

If you want to know what is offensive in this world, it's the sight of two sweaty male college students sitting shirtless in a four-and-a-half-mat tatami room glaring at each other. At that moment, the scorching sun was broiling the roof of Shimogamo Yusuiso, and the displeasure index inside room 209 had reached its peak. With zero shame or concern for my reputation, I left the window and door open, but even when I turned on the basically antique fan I brought from my parents' house, it only pushed the hot air around the room; I was so warm my consciousness was growing fuzzy. Did the man squatting before me really exist? He wasn't a grimy mirage only purehearted I could see?

Mopping my sweat with a hand towel, I spoke to him. "Hey, Ozu."

". . . You rang?"

"Are you alive?"

"Oh, don't mind me. I'll be dead before long," he said with a cold stare. His grayish, unhealthy-looking face was slick with sweat, which made him gleam slimily—he looked just like a freshly birthed Nurarihyon.

The student apartments were peaceful and quiet in the afternoon. The cicada cries that had been obnoxiously loud in the morning had ceased altogether, and the silence made it feel as though the flow of time had stopped. Many residents had gone home to their families; not many idiots spent midsummer days cooped up in a four-and-a-half-mat tatami room.

Probably the only other person in the ramshackle building aside from Ozu and me was my neighbor in room 210, the perpetual student Seitaro Higuchi. The previous night, we had solemnly held a wake for my air conditioner. At dawn, Higuchi snakily intoned an error-riddled version of the Heart Sutra before blurting, "If you clear your mind, even a four-and-a-half-mat tatami room is as refreshing as Karuizawa—*katsu*!" as if to jolt us toward enlightenment as he repaired to the room next door. We hadn't seen him since. I was amazed he could sleep so soundly in this hellish heat.

Ozu said he wanted a mango Frappuccino, so I poured

some salty, lukewarm barley tea into a little cup for him. Ozu slurped it like an ill toad sipping muddy water.

"Ahh, this is awful . . . just awful . . ."

"Shut up and drink it."

"I'm sick of getting my minerals the same way they did in the Edo period."

I ignored his sad moaning.

Earlier, I wrote "a wake for my air conditioner."

It's only natural that some of you wise readers would dubiously wonder what that was supposed to mean.

The air conditioner we mourned throughout the night was a fabled appliance that had been installed in room 209 in ancient times. The civilized convenience, so at odds with the atmosphere of a four-and-a-half-mat tatami room, was almost surely installed without the landlord's permission; it was a historic heritage that spoke volumes to that former resident's great courage. As the only four-and-a-half-mat tatami room in the building with an air conditioner, 209 had become the envy of all the residents.

I first heard rumors of room 209 two summers ago. A longtime student wearing only his briefs, whom I encountered in the common-use kitchen, whispered into my ear as I sweat, "My good sir, apparently this building has a four-and-a-half-mat tatami room with an air conditioner." At the time, the "four-and-a-half-mat tatami room with an air conditioner" that the student—who introduced himself as Seitaro Higuchi—mentioned sounded like some kind of far-off dreamland, like the legendary isle of Avalon where King Arthur is said to have spent his final days. I never imagined I would have the honor of moving into it two years later.

But despite moving from the first floor to the second expressly for the air conditioner, I was able to benefit for only a handful of days.

That was all the fault of the man before me, Ozu.

• • •

Ozu was in the same year as me. Despite being registered in the Department of Electric and Electronic Engineering, he hated electricity, electronics, and engineering. At the end of freshman year he had received so few credits, and with such low grades, that it made you wonder whether there was any point to him being there.

Because he hated vegetables and ate only instant foods, his face was such a creepy color it looked like he'd been living on the far side of the moon. Eight out of ten people who met him walking down the street at night would take him for a yokai goblin. The other two would be shape-shifted yokai themselves. Ozu kicked those who were down and buttered up anyone stronger than him. He was selfish and arrogant, lazy and contrary. He never studied, had not a crumb of pride, and fueled himself on other people's misfortunes. There was not a single praiseworthy bone in his body. If only I had never met him, my soul would surely be less tainted.

"I can't believe you ruined my life."

"But all I did was spill Coke on your remote." Ozu wiped his slimy face and cackled. "I'm sure Akashi'll figure something out for you."

"The point is, you should think about what you've done."

"Why should I have to do that?" His expression said he found the suggestion entirely unjust. "This is what they call joint liability. Saying we should film a movie here was Akashi's bad, leaving the remote where you did was your bad, and the one who left out a half-drunk bottle of Coke was in the wrong, too. The one most at fault is the one who declared, 'I'm going to get naked and dance'—which was you."

"I don't recall saying anything like that."

"There's no getting out of it now. You worked us all into a frenzy, didn't you? Anyway," he continued blabbing, "if the whole thing becomes inoperable just because some Coke got spilled on the remote, that's pretty shoddy design. Yet here you are trying to put all the blame on me—'think about what you've done'? I'm the one who's the victim here!"

The Nurarihyon had a point: it was strange that the unit itself didn't have any buttons. If Akashi's attempt to get the remote repaired failed, we would have lost the only way to turn on the air conditioner, and I would have to spend the rest of the summer in a broiling four-and-a-half-mat tatami room. Agh, if I had known this would happen, I wouldn't have moved. It was cooler on the first floor.

I stood up, wrung my hand towel out in the sink, and put it over my shoulder.

"This year I was finally supposed to have a meaningful summer. I was supposed to escape this depraved lifestyle and turn over a new leaf as a good man. That's what the air conditioner was for!"

"Nah, your prospects there are nonexistent," Ozu replied.

"How dare you!"

"I'll do everything in my power to corrupt you, you know. What does an air conditioner have to do with leading a meaningful student life, anyway? I won't have you underestimating me."

I sat back down and glared at him. "You find this funny, don't you?"

"I'll leave that to your imagination, ooh-hoo-hoo."

Ozu and I met our freshman year in the imaginary train club known as the Keifuku Electric Railroad Research Society. In the two and a half years since, Ozu had been standing in every dark corner of my embarrassing youth. A Mephistopheles leading students with bright futures to a barren wasteland, that's what he was. Spilling Coke on the remote could very well have been part of his plot. After all, he was a man who fueled himself on other people's misfortunes.

I whipped him with my wet hand towel. "How about showing some semblance of remorse?!"

"The word 'remorse' isn't in my dictionary. *Heh-heh-heh*," Ozu chuckled, whipping me back with his own hand towel.

As we got into a rhythm, exchanging blows—"You little—!" "I hardly felt that!"—we started having fun. Having smacked each other's meager physiques for a time, Ozu finally shrieked, "Uheegh!" and curled into a ball.

"Oh, you surrender?" I said whipping him even more vigorously, and he put up his hands and screamed, "Hold up, time out! Someone's here!"

When I turned around, I found Akashi standing outside the open door. She had a big bag over her left shoulder and a bottle of ramune in her right hand. She was watching us with the

9

earnest gaze of an elementary-schooler absorbed in observing morning glories.

"Oh, the idiocy of friendship," she murmured, taking a slug of her soda.

• • •

Akashi was a year behind us. She belonged to the Ablutions film club, and contrary to her cool appearance, she was a lovable character who mass-produced absolutely uncool, trashy movies. According to Ozu, who was also an Ablutions member, even within the club, people weren't sure how to appraise her as a director. No praise was spared for her utterly professional work ethic that saw her film three projects in the time others did one, but when it came time to touch on what garbage they all were, everyone modestly zipped their lips.

Paying no mind to the hazy estimation from her peers, Akashi set about producing a storm of work fit for literary giant Balzac, if he had been reborn into the world of bad cinema. The previous day from early morning until after three p.m., she had filmed a lame sci-fi-slash-period-flick at the landlady's house, which was located behind the apartment building.

Akashi put her bag down in the doorway of the four-and-a-half-mat tatami room. "What were you doing?"

"Nothing."

"We're going insane from the heat, ooh-hoo-hoo."

"For a second I thought it was some kind of sex act. It seemed like something I shouldn't be watching, but the door was wide open . . ."

"It *was* an act of love."

"Anyway, please forget it, Akashi."

"Understood. I'll forget it. I've forgotten it."

Ozu and I hurried to make ourselves presentable, and Akashi quietly entered the room.

Was the old man at the electronics store able to bring the remote back from its baptism in loathsome Coke? As I watched with bated breath, Akashi sat upright and pressed her palms together: "I'm sorry for your loss."

I felt all the energy leave my body. "So there was nothing he could do?"

"I left the remote with him, but he told me it would be pretty much impossible. It's an old model—so old he was surprised to know someone was still using it. He said it was definitely time to buy a new unit."

"If I could do that, I wouldn't have this problem."

"Right."

Ozu leaned back arrogantly and said, "Well, Akashi, I'm very disappointed in you."

"You shut up for the rest of infinity."

"No, it's just as he says. I'm filled with regret," said Akashi.

Apparently, she had spent a constructive half day of summer before coming over.

She rose at seven thirty and greeted the morning sun, ate a nutritious breakfast and headed to school, arrived at the university library as it opened and studied there for two hours; then she not only went around to electronics shops to get the remote repaired, but even stopped by the Kyoto Antiquarian Book Fair in Tadasu no Mori at Shimogamo Shrine.

What had we been doing while Akashi was having such a productive morning? Sitting cross-legged in a sweltering four-and-a-half-mat tatami room glaring at each other and producing nothing but sweat. Fruitless. Foolish. The hell of this world. A summertime I could never get back was melting away like a dish of shaved ice left out in the sun. It was too futile for words.

Akashi inquired in surprise, "Ozu, did you end up staying here?"

"We were mourning the air conditioner all night!" he said proudly. "This was the room every resident pined for, so everyone came by to unload their silent fury. Though I was fine, of course."

"Because you're such a weirdo."

"You would know, dear sister in disciplehood," said Ozu.

"Thanks to you, my life plans are in shambles," I told him.

"But don't we have fun wasting our days on pointless bullshit? What are you complaining about?"

I was wringing Ozu's neck as he laughed when some squeaking and static echoed in the hallway.

Shimogamo Yusuiso was equipped with speakers connected to the landlady's house. They were located above the glass door that led to the laundry-drying area at the end of the hall on each floor to deliver the elderly woman's gracious words to all her tenants. Coming through the worn-out speakers, her voice took on a dignified tone, as if it were descending from the celestial realm, so it was customarily known as the "Voice of the Heavens." Generally it was reminding people to pay their rent.

"Higuchi? Calling Seitaro Higuchi in 210." The landlady's

solemn voice echoed in the hallway. "I know you're in your room. Please come pay your rent."

But there was no sign of my strange neighbor awakening. The Voice of the Heavens repeated its message a couple times in vain before stopping, and the apartment building was silent again.

"He didn't react at all!"

"Unwakeable as a mountain."

"So Master's still asleep? I'd expect nothing less," said Akashi.

As hard as it is to believe, Akashi was a "disciple" of Higuchi's along with Ozu, so she had been visiting the building since the end of the previous year.

Certainly, he was treated with respect by the residents as the "master" of the building, and even the landlady paid him a degree of respect.

But from my perspective, as someone who had observed his lifestyle in detail over the previous two and a half years, I could say that Seitaro Higuchi was the living crystallization of that old stereotype of a thickheaded perpetual student—a most hazardous pilot, who would navigate you straight into one of life's cul-de-sacs. I kept thinking, *Please don't waste your precious youth seeking wisdom from such an inscrutable guy*, but I couldn't help but wholeheartedly welcome Akashi's visits to this dump of a building, so I'd been watching over her this half a year with extremely complicated feelings.

I drained my barley tea and said, "What is Higuchi even a master *of*?"

"A question that strikes to the heart of things. To be honest, I don't know, either."

"If I had to say, I suppose it'd be something like a 'master of life'?" said Akashi.

"Nice, Akashi," said Ozu with a nod. "If you're just gonna hole up in this four-and-a-half-mat tatami room unable to commit to anything, you should be a disciple, too. You've got time to kill now that you've been chased out of the Keifuku Electric Railroad Research Society, right? Actually, I suggested making you a disciple the other day, and our master readily approved. So really, you already are one."

"What the heck? You didn't even ask me."

"It's fine, it's fine. Don't be shy."

Then Akashi peered into my face and said, "It's fun, actually. Why don't you join us?"

That one sweet word was enough to fell even me and my iron will.

If I became a disciple of Higuchi, Akashi would automatically become my elder sister in disciplehood. *Elder sister in disciplehood!* What an alluring ring that had to it. It sounded as sweet as the silkiest ankoro mochi.

But I was neither seeking an elder sister in disciplehood—even if she fell into my lap like a piece of botamochi falling from a shelf—nor did I have any desire to learn about life from that inscrutable weirdo. I wanted to assertively obtain a meaningful summer, not just brattily content myself with fruitless, idle days. Then, once I had turned over a new leaf . . .

I glanced at Akashi before answering, "No, I refuse to be a disciple."

"Bummer." Ozu heaved an exaggerated sigh. "If you were a disciple, I was going to invite you to watch the Gozan Okuribi on the sixteenth. Master is going to take us to a secret place with a fantastic view—it's an invaluable opportunity. But whatever. You can just hug your knees on your tatami and watch them on KBS Kyoto. Akashi, you should keep your schedule free."

"I'm not going," said Akashi.

Ozu's eyes went wide. "Huh? Why? What's up?"

"I promised I'd go with someone else."

"You didn't say anything about that yesterday. Who the heck are you going with?"

"Why should I have to tell you?" she said flatly, staring him in the face.

Not even Ozu had anything to say to that. It felt amazing—a booyah moment if there ever was one—but to tell the truth, I was also destroyed in that instant.

On August 16, Akashi was going out to watch the ritual fires burn. With *who*, though?

When I stole a glance at her profile, she had the most chill look on her face. It was as if she were standing in Tadasu no Mori in the middle of winter; I couldn't see a single bead of sweat on her fair cheeks.

"Akashi, aren't you warm?" I asked.

"I'm extremely warm," she said as she downed the rest of her ramune.

• • •

A new project had begun filming the morning of the previous day (August 11), *Lives of Bakumatsu Weaklings: Samurai Wars.*

Just from the trashy title, you can get an idea of the rich trashiness of this movie. Ozu and I had come up with the concept. Akashi took an interest in the stupid convos we were having on my tatami mats, and before we knew it, she had written a script and said, "I want to make this into a movie."

In the latter days of the Tokugawa shogunate, the Keio era . . .

By some strange turn of events, university student Susumu Ginga has time-slipped from his twenty-first-century, four-and-a-half-mat tatami room and wandered into the hideout of the Meiji Restoration patriots. There he meets Saigo Takamori, Sakamoto Ryoma, Takasugi Shinsaku, Iwakura Tomomi, Katsu Kaishu, Hijikata Toshizo, and other famous figures of Bakumatsu and Restoration history.

Ginga, however, has a fearsome power: he turns everyone he meets into useless slackers.

Under his influence, the Bakumatsu men lose their drive, one after the other, and both factions, that in support of the shogunate and that overthrowing it, rapidly collapse. By the time he worries, "At this rate, the future will change!" it's too late, and even when he goes around warning of the dangers of altering history, the Bakumatsu men only chuckle merrily, "Ah-ha-ha!"

Before long, the supporters and overthrowers come together in a wild dance, chanting, "*E ja nai ka, e ja nai ka*"—"Who cares?" Unable to withstand the considerable alteration to history, the space-time continuum undergoes a massive collapse, and tragically, the universe is destroyed. What a pity.

That is all; the end.

When I looked over the script, I couldn't help but murmur, "Are you sure about this?"

"Yes," Akashi nodded firmly. "I'm sure."

The previous morning, streams of students had gathered at Shimogamo Yusuiso.

They were the members of the film club Akashi belonged to, Ablutions.

In this crowd of amateur filmmakers, there was one man who was more self-important than all the rest: the club's boss, Jogasaki. Clicking his tongue as he barged in—"This building isn't fit for human habitation"—he not only lingered in room 209 (which I had offered as a greenroom) as if he owned the place, but even committed the violent act of blasting the air conditioning with the door open. It goes without saying that the electricity meter, whirling with a force I had neither seen nor heard before, had turned into a barometer of my rage. On top of that, Jogasaki started loudly pointing out how trashy Akashi's script was.

Certainly, his assertion was correct. It was worth listening to. *But you're the last person I want to hear that from.*

"I came up with the concept, actually," I said. The reason I was assisting with the filming despite not being a member of the club was that I felt a sense of responsibility as the creator.

"Oh really? Huh." Jogasaki looked at me.

His attitude said, *And? What about it?*

This was the moment the clash between Jogasaki and me became decisive.

From now on, I will think only of hindering this character, and in the wickedest possible ways. For starters, I set the air conditioner to heater mode and left the room.

The second floor had been crowded with all sorts of junk

to begin with, so with the cast and crew piled in, it was like a packed train. Akashi flitted around like a honeybee, completely absorbed in costume checks and other various consultations. I was admiring her valiant profile when I heard Jogasaki scream from 209, "Why is the heat on?!"—which was immensely gratifying.

At that moment, the door to 210 opened, and Seitaro Higuchi showed his face.

"Hello, my good sir," he said to me.

Higuchi had his grown-out hair tied back and his arms in the breast of a dark green yukata instead of through the sleeves. This was a costume for the movie, but it wasn't much different from how he usually appeared around the building. Stroking his chin, which looked like a big eggplant coated in iron filings, he sunnily proclaimed, "*Nippon no yoake zeyo!* It's the dawn of Japan!"

"You're playing Sakamoto Ryoma?"

"Indeed. I can't refuse a disciple's request." He drew a model gun out of the breast of his yukata. "Nippon no yoake zeyo! Nippon no yoake zeyo!"

Just as a creepy person with a white-painted face was coming down the hall, I realized it was Ozu made up as Iwakura Tomomi. Shielding his mouth with a shining golden fan, he wriggled his body indecently, obnoxiously shouting, "*Ojaru!* Ojaru!*" Higuchi retorted by pointing the barrel of the model gun at Ozu and screaming, "Yoake zeyo! Yoake zeyo!" which was about when a disgruntled Jogasaki dressed as Saigo Takamori came out of room 209 and started saying, "*Gowasu,* gowasu," adding to the chaos of period-speak.

For the filming, we borrowed the landlady's house out back. Her eyes went wide as the parade of students poured in. "Oh, my, this is quite the production."

The crew set up camp in a tatami room with an engawa porch facing the yard.

Beyond the yard's trees, the apartment building's shabby laundry-drying area was in plain view, but if we figured out a way to avoid getting that in the frame, this could totally pass as the Restoration patriots' hideout.

What caught my eye was the stone sculpture in one corner of the yard. It was a strange statue of a beefy, humanoid yokai sitting cross-legged, and it brought to mind H. P. Lovecraft's horror stories. Apparently it was a statue of the kappa master of the swamp that used to be in this area. "If we don't treat it well, we'll be cursed," the landlady repeatedly warned us, so we couldn't move it.

Akashi gazed at the statue and murmured, "It looks sort of like Jogasaki, don't you think?"

Indeed, its brawny physique bore a strong resemblance to Jogasaki.

Playing the role of Susumu Ginga, the blockheaded university student who time-slips from a twenty-first-century, four-and-a-half-mat tatami room, was an upperclassman from Ablutions, Aijima. He was a slim man who put on airs with a pair of smart specs, and the fake-polite, sweet-talking voice he used when addressing Akashi offended me.

Like Jogasaki, Aijima constantly pointed out what garbage the script was. He found fault with trivial actions the protagonist took, grumbling, "I can't act this because it doesn't make sense to me psychologically."

Unable to put up with his complaining, I countered: "It'll never turn out if you're whining the whole time."

"I've been wondering for a while now, Who the heck are you even? Where'd you come from?" Aijima said coldly, narrowing his eyes behind his glasses.

"I'm just a helpful passerby."

"Nobody asked your opinion."

"I came up with the concept."

"Oh, is that right? Huh." Aijima looked at me.

His attitude said, *And? What about it?*

Nobody, not Jogasaki, not Aijima, nobody could understand what Akashi was trying to do, nor did they try to. They were so full of themselves.

Raging along those lines, I got to thinking: *Aren't I exactly the same?*

I was assisting with the filming vainly convinced that some thoughtful advice from me would improve Akashi's trashy movie. Did she even once say to me, "Please improve my trashy movie"?

It was precisely a trashy movie that Akashi wanted to make. Then shouldn't I be stubbornly protecting the film's lovable trashiness from those fools who would scheme to make improvements? It was by cultivating tight bonds with Akashi over the course of that fight that I would escape the fate of a pebble by the wayside.

I quietly resolved to make that my policy.

Akashi stood on the engawa and announced that filming would begin: "Okay, everyone. Let's get started."

As it turned out, my quiet resolve wasn't very useful.

Ever since the Lumière brothers invented the cinematograph, there has surely never been a movie that completed filming without incident. Even if every grain of sand vanished from the shore, there would still be filming incidents.

None of the bizarre bunch of actors followed instructions. Jogasaki, ever discontent with his role as Saigo Takamori, kept rewriting his lines; Aijima was preoccupied with his expression of his character's mental state and kept demanding retakes; Ozu writhing around in whiteface was so disgusting he was unfilmable; and Higuchi refused to say any lines besides "It's the dawn of Japan!"

The Shinsengumi fellows were all so into their roles that they had grown irritable and cold, and a sword fight broke out over the bento lunches. The sound person and the lighting person erupted in a lover's quarrel; the landlady's dog, Kecha, burst onto the set; and a number of club members left a note and disappeared because they were fed up with all the issues. During a fight scene, Ozu knocked over the kappa statue and got an earful from the landlady.

Nevertheless, Akashi used every trick in the book to continue filming. The script was revised over and over, characters were swapped in and out, the filming order was changed. She didn't even hesitate to lie, if it would convince the actors. Sometimes what she said was a rehearsal was the real deal, while other times what she said was the real deal turned out to be a rehearsal; sometimes she said, "We'll retake it later," and then never did.

Is this film headed for collapse or completion? Not one person involved knew the answer—except Akashi.

Just past three o'clock, after the actors all danced like a mob of zombies chanting, "E ja nai ka," Akashi announced that filming had wrapped, but no one believed her. Silence reigned. Next to the cast, who all just stood there in an absentminded daze, Kecha was taking a solemn dump.

"Seems like it'll be an interesting movie." Higuchi's comment rang hollow.

After a little while, Ozu asked Akashi, "Are we really done?"

"Yes, that's a wrap. Thanks for your hard work."

"It seems like we skipped a lot . . ."

"No, we got everything we needed." Akashi replied, unconcerned. "The rest I'll handle in post."

Was that possible?

Was the film really complete?

I thought to say, *Akashi*, but held my tongue.

She stood alone in the yard looking up at the bright sky.

At that moment, she appeared more satisfied than I'd ever seen her.

• • •

"Are you okay?"

Akashi's voice brought me back to myself. I guess I had spaced out due to the heat.

The events of yesterday, flickering across the back of my mind like shadows cast by a revolving lantern, overwhelmed me, like a major motion picture filmed in Technicolor. I had never in my life spent such a densely packed time. But that wasn't all that happened during that long day.

After filming, I had gone with Higuchi, Ozu, and some other guys to the bathhouse Oasis before checking out the Shimogamo Shrine used book fair, and when I got back to the apartment building, the Coke Incident happened, and my air conditioner breathed its last. The longest day in rotten university student history drew to a close with the appliance's gloomy, depressing wake.

"Long day yesterday," I sighed, and Akashi bobbed her head.

"Thanks to you, we were able to finish filming," said Akashi.

"Is that how it always goes?"

"The scale has never been that large, but it's always chaos, yes. Still, I prefer it that way. Adds some wacky flavor."

"I thought it would never be finished."

"How come?" she looked at me strangely. "As long as we film something, we can shape it up in the editing room."

"Akashi is second to none when it comes to having the muscle to complete a film," Ozu crowed. "Of course, the end result is always trash."

"Hey, don't call it trash," I said.

"I mean, it's trash, though."

"It's fine for it to be trash. That's what I'm going for," said Akashi, and Ozu gave me a look: *See?*

Every November for the school festival, the Ablutions film club borrowed a room in one of the school buildings and put on the Ablutions Film Festival. The goal was to screen *Lives of Bakumatsu Weaklings* at this festival. The problem was that detestable upperclassman, Jogasaki. He was the one who made the final calls on the lineup, and he had already expressed his intentions to weed out trash. The chances he would like *Lives of Bakumatsu Weaklings* were low, and in the worst case, he might refuse to screen it.

"He's such a tyrant!" I was furious when I heard about this from Akashi, but Ozu was nonchalant.

"We can just ask Hanuki. Not even Jogasaki can refuse her a favor."

Hanuki was a dental hygienist employed at Kubozuka Dental in the neighborhood.

Apparently Higuchi, Jogasaki, and Hanuki went way back. She sometimes came to visit Higuchi, so I had exchanged words with her before. She was a beautiful woman who greeted me, in cheerful approximations of English, "Good morning" or "Good night" every time we met in the hallway. She had shown up just as filming was finishing the previous day, too, moving the camera without asking, messing with Ozu's face paint, giving notes on Higuchi's acting—swaggering around as usual. She was a bit over the top, but it was impossible to dislike her.

"I suppose," said Akashi after thinking for a moment. "But I doubt we need to go that far. I've made a ton of movies up to this point, and I'm going to keep on making them. With so many to look at, Jogasaki's bound to overlook one. He can't reject them all."

"Ah yes, the strategy of overwhelming your opponent with matériel might," I groaned.

"Let me know if you have any other good movie ideas."

In any case, I was glad that Akashi seemed satisfied. It reminded me of the way she had gazed up at the sky after filming with that fulfilled look on her face.

I was happy that the idea born of my and Ozu's bullshitting had been useful to her. But that fact brought a shade of sadness to my breast.

Akashi would create a film (trash though it may be) based on our pointless bullshitting. But what had *I* accomplished during the past two and a half years of student-hood? Following the misery of being banished from the Keifuku Electric Railroad Research Society, I had lost all faith in the world and holed up in the minute galaxy of my four-and-a-half-mat tatami room—my only visitor, the half-yokai Ozu.

The riot of blooming bullshit bore no fruit, petals uselessly falling to the tatami floor. Where would continuing in this vein get me?

As long as I didn't forge myself into an individual fit for society, I would never be qualified to stand at Akashi's side. That was the whole point of acquiring this elusive treasure, the air conditioner of which rumors had been passed down over the years.

I looked up regretfully at the air conditioner: "Ahh, AC!"

"You don't know when to give up either, huh?"

"I'm never going to forgive you as long as I live."

"Even if you never forgive me, our friendship will live forever," said Ozu. "We're connected by the black thread of fate."

The horrific image of two men, bound like boneless hams

by a dark thread, sinking to dark watery depths, came to mind, and I shuddered.

"You guys really get along." Akashi smiled.

• • •

Ozu I didn't care about, but I couldn't bear to make Akashi sit in the excessively hot four-and-a-half-mat tatami room.

I suggested that we go out into the hallway: "It should be a little cooler there."

But it wasn't as if we stepped into a refreshing stretch of scenery just by exiting my room.

Across the hall was the building's storage closet, and the junk overflowing from it was piled up outside: supplies the weekly cleaning lady used, furniture that must have been abandoned by previous residents, the landlady's personal property . . . the mess had achieved such harmony that it would be impossible to clean up, so even the landlady must have been pretending not to see it. The first time I came upon this scene, I thought someone was barricading off the second-floor hallway—that's how bad it was.

Akashi sat on a couch that was leaking yellow stuffing.

Ozu was knocking on number 210, next door.

"Good not-morning-anymore, Master. Good not-morning-anymore!"

After a moment, we heard Seitaro Higuchi mumbling inside.

". . . If you . . ."

"If you?"

". . . clear your mind . . ."

"Clear your mind?"

". . . even a four-and-a-half-mat tatami room is as refreshing as Kamikochi!"

Room 210 fell silent once more.

I went out to the laundry-drying area for some air.

Having made my way through the dirty-looking laundry, I leaned against the railing. Below, I could see the simple shower that had been built on the property and rods for hanging clothes. The concrete wall in the back was adjacent to the landlady's spacious yard, and the leafy trees gleamed in the summer sun. The engawa facing the green lawn looked so nice and cool, and Kecha, the landlady's dog, was lying beneath it.

"Hey, Kecha!"

I called him just to fool around, and he sluggishly moved just his head to look up. But he didn't know what direction he had been called from, so after a moment's blank stare, he snorted as if to say, *Guess it was my imagination*, and rested his head back on the ground.

This lovable mutt had made it his life's work to dig holes any and everywhere. When he wasn't digging holes, he was either napping lazily under the porch as he was now or chasing his tail in circles. Whenever I saw this carefree dog, I thought of the philosopher Schopenhauer's famous quote about how animals are "the present moment personified." As the notion of time dissolved for me as a result of my fruitless tatami-room life, I started thinking maybe I was more like a dog than a human, so I always felt like calling out to Kecha, *O precious neighbor pup!*

Yesterday, excited by the crowd of students that had barged into the landlady's house to film, Kecha had dug more holes, run in more circles, and defecated with even more freedom than usual. He was zooming around so much that we were forced to accept him as an extra. "Dogs existed during the Bakumatsu period, too," said Akashi.

"Kecha!" I tried calling him one more time, but the precious pup didn't move another muscle.

When I returned to the hallway from the laundry-drying area, Akashi was seated on the couch, staring at a computer open in her lap. Ozu was sitting in the hall, rapturously soaking his feet in a little tub of water.

"Hey, don't abuse my bath bucket," I said.

"Don't worry," he said without opening his eyes. "My feet are as pure as a newborn's."

As I was standing there miffed, Akashi showed us the previous day's footage on her computer. Ozu wriggling with his white makeup was creepy, and the discontent Jogasaki felt about his role was clear from his sulky face. Despite having been so concerned about the psychological aspects of his character, Aijima delivered his lines in an absolute monotone. About the rest of the cast, I could only assume that they were possessed by the ghosts of bad actors.

"This is awful. Truly awful." Ozu set aside his own performance and laughed his ass off.

But Seitaro Higuchi actually achieved an impressive presence. Though his only line was "It's the dawn of Japan!" the nuance changed depending on the scene and provided the film with a common thread.

Given the tragic end, wherein time traveler Susumu Ginga's alteration of history causes the universe to collapse and everyone is fresh out of fucks to give about the "dawn of Japan," Higuchi's repeated line took on an ironic, grim tone. There's no way Higuchi could have planned to express that, so if this effect was Akashi's idea, she was really a force to be reckoned with.

As I was inwardly admiring her, the kappa statue appeared on the screen. The more I looked at it, the creepier it got. I don't know how the landlady felt about keeping it in her garden and looking out at it every day; maybe she wanted to get rid of it but couldn't, for fear of the curse.

"I wonder why he's so muscular."

"Kappa are said to love sumo, right? Perhaps he works out," Akashi replied.

"At the bottom of the swamp?"

"Yes, at the bottom of the swamp. Like, maybe he's a body-builder," she murmured in seriousness before smiling. "Still, it's funny how much he looks like Jogasaki."

We watched the video for a time. White-faced Iwakura Tomomi (that is, Ozu) ran around the yard and eventually leaped at the statue of the kappa. Then the Shinsengumi flooded in with a clear lack of discipline. As they struggled like elementary-schoolers on Sports Day, the kappa statue tipped over in slow motion.

This accident enraged the landlady, and we had no choice but to stop filming.

"I'm glad no one got hurt."

"Akashi." I pointed at the screen. "You can see the laundry-drying area."

"Oh, yeah. I'll do something about it in post."

Just then she leaned toward the screen with a puzzled look on her face and a "Huh?" but I didn't think anything of it. A man coming down the hall had caught my attention.

He stopped midway and timidly inquired, "Umm, excuse me. You live here, right?"

A dorky mushroom of a haircut, a dorky T-shirt stuffed into dorky pants—even the bag slung across his body was dorky. It was as if he were a missionary from the Kingdom of Dorkiness come to spread dorkiness throughout the land— all I could feel toward his thorough unfashionableness was affinity as a fellow dork. *He has some good qualities*, I thought.

"Did you just move in?" I asked.

"No . . ."

"Oh, then are you looking for someone?"

"No, not exactly . . ."

Dorky's embarrassed expression seemed to say he didn't know how to proceed. He blushed red and clammed up. Akashi looked up from her computer, puzzled.

The awkward silence was broken by the Voice of the Heavens.

"Higuchi? Seitaro Higuchi in room 210." The landlady's solemn voice echoed in the hallway. "I know you're in your room. Please come pay your rent."

Dorky's eyes went wide and he looked up at the speaker.

"What's that?"

"The landlady's PA system."

"PA system? Ah, just like the stories . . ."

His eyes gleamed, but I had no idea what he was so emotional about.

Just then, the door of room 210 finally opened in response to the Voice of the Heavens. The one who sluggishly emerged from the darkness was the most long-term resident of the apartment building, whispered about as the "Guardian Deity of Four-and-a-Half-Mat Tatami Rooms," as well as a "tengu who crashed into a four-and-a-half-mat tatami room by accident": Seitaro Higuchi. The disheveled hair on his head stretched skyward like the bristles of a broom stood on its handle, the yukata he wore couldn't get any shabbier, and sweat dripped from the tip of his huge chin.

"Hello, my good sir. It's another rather hot day, isn't it?" Higuchi said, wiping himself down with a damp hand towel.

Just then Dorky shrieked in amazement, "Master Higuchi! You're here, too? How?"

Higuchi looked at Dorky with sleepy eyes—not seeming particularly suspicious.

"I just went with the flow and ended up here."

"With the flow?"

"Indeed." Higuchi nodded. "Now then, who might you be?"

But Dorky didn't answer. He worked his mouth in silence like a moronic goldfish, looking at each of us in turn, and then said in a tiny voice, "Sorry to have bothered you," turned on his heel, and ran off. The pattering of his footsteps retreated down the hallway and continued down the stairs.

Akashi said, "Do you know him?"

"No, I don't recall ever meeting him."

"But he seemed to know your name, Master."

"Perhaps we brushed sleeves somewhere in this floating world. The current of people never ceases flowing, yet the people are never the same . . . I've just met so many people," he said in a carefree tone as he stroked his unshaven chin.

•   •   •

I wasn't a fan of this Seitaro Higuchi guy.

We may have lived in the same building, but I did my best to keep my distance from this perpetual student. My animal instincts told me he was a dangerous character.

Higuchi fanned himself with his rent stamp book.

Rent in this building was paid according to the outdated system of handing cash to the landlady, who then gave us a stamp. Higuchi's book was so financially battle-worn, it looked like a historical document discovered in an Edo-period storehouse.

"I'm going to go pay rent. Yet I have no money," Higuchi said calmly as if he were stating a scientific fact. "I have no money. Yet I'm going to go pay rent." We were still stunned when he said, "By the way," changing the topic, "who took my Vidal Sassoon?"

"Vidal Sassoon?"

We all cocked our heads.

"You mean your shampoo?"

Higuchi answered Akashi's question. "Yes. If you want to turn yourself in, now is the time. If you confess, I'll consider it water under the bridge."

Apparently Higuchi's beloved Vidal Sassoon Base Care

Moisture Control Shampoo had vanished from his toiletries kit at some point. I could set aside the unexpected fussiness regarding the texture of his hair, but I couldn't let him assume one of us had committed the crime.

"Who would steal shampoo?" I said.

"No, no. This is some great shampoo we're talking about." He pointed at his towering hairs as if to say, *Just look at this luster!* All I could grasp was that Higuchi put his full trust in Vidal Sassoon.

"It must be the work of this guy, as usual." When I balled up the accusation like a wet kimono and hurled it at Ozu, he nimbly dodged.

"I would never betray the master."

"You all went to the bathhouse yesterday, didn't you? Did you have the shampoo on your way home?" Akashi asked.

"Oh." Higuchi stared into space. "Now that you mention it, I get the feeling that maybe I didn't."

"So perhaps you forgot it at the bathhouse. Why don't you call Oasis and ask? I'm sure the custodian is holding it for you."

With Akashi's offer of such an unassailable solution, the meaningless exchange brought on by Higuchi's baseless deductions came to an end.

"Well, I suppose I'll go pay rent, then," Higuchi said and went walking slowly down the hallway. Ozu immediately jogged over to his side.

"Master, allow me to accompany you."

"You'll be my backup?"

"I sure will. See? Who's a more loyal disciple than me?"

Apparently Ozu meant to pay Higuchi's rent for him.

The landlady's house was adjacent to the rear of the apartment building. To go there, you had to go out the apartment building's front entrance and follow a stone path around to the house's entrance. But whenever you paid rent, you would be treated to tea and snacks, so it always took a while to get your stamp.

In other words, Higuchi and Ozu wouldn't be back for a while.

I leaned against the hallway's wall and watched over Akashi, who was still on the couch.

A breeze blew in from the laundry-drying area and rang the wind chime. Since we had been in the stifling tatami room until a moment ago, it felt as cool as the wind in Kamikochi.

"This feels extremely 'summer vacation,' don't you think?" Akashi looked up and closed her eyes. "Like nostalgic, somehow."

Now that she mentioned it, I did have that feeling.

It was like one of those childhood afternoons after you'd spent all morning swimming at the pool—gazing at the languid sunshine while eating ice cream or something, the comfortable exhaustion-inducing drowsiness. A sweet feeling mixed with melancholy, empty yet fulfilled, wells up. But the space-time of summer vacation stretches out before you like a blank canvas. Even as an elementary-schooler, I felt it keenly: *This must be that thing called happiness.*

As I absorbed myself in those reminiscences, the deserted apartment building began to feel like a summer poolside of long ago.

A summer afternoon alone with Akashi.

Stop, O time. It was only natural to want to pray.

With no way to know of my inward prayer, Akashi was staring at her computer with a frown and a slight stoop. She must have been thinking about her editing.

As I stared, fascinated by her valiant profile, her exchange with Ozu regarding the Gozan Okuribi came to mind. My heart flew into an uncontrollable panic. It felt as though I was seeing an ominous dark cloud pressing in from beyond the horizon.

Akashi would go out to watch the ceremonial fires on August 16.

With who, exactly?!

To me, this was a major issue, one that was impossible to ignore.

• • •

Here I'd like to move the hands of time back one day again, to August 11.

After filming, we went to the bathhouse Oasis.

We exited the building into the scorching hot residential neighborhood just after four p.m. The sun cast dark shadows at our feet, and cicadas were crying in the trees lining the street.

I felt like I was having déjà vu.

How many of these same languorous afternoons had we spent this summer?

The closest bathhouse, Oasis, was down Mikage-dori away

from Shimogamo Izumikawacho and across the Takano River to the east, in a residential area. Between the curtain with just the character *yu*—for bathwater—left undyed, the elevated custodian's seat, and the big baskets lined up in the changing rooms, it was truly the Platonic ideal of a public bathhouse.

Shimogamo Yusuiso had only a coin-operated shower that cost a hundred yen for ten minutes, so any residents who wanted to take a leisurely soak crossed the Mikagebashi Bridge to head to Oasis. As its name implied, this bathhouse was an oasis for many wandering four-and-a-half-mat-tatami-ists.

We spaced out soaking in the large tub.

"*Chu chu tako kai na.*" Ozu sang a strange song.

"*Lives of Bakumatsu Weaklings* seems like it'll be a pretty interesting movie, huh?" I said.

"I think not." Jogasaki groaned.

"Oh? You're not happy with it, Jogasaki?"

"How could I be? I'll never approve of such a trashy movie."

"Akashi was pretty satisfied."

"A film is an appeal to society and should be made with more sincerity. The script alone was a shit show. You're making a mockery of the people around you by even thinking about making a movie out of that. I think she's wasting her talent."

"I mean, it's an amateur film either way."

"Guys like you are going to send our culture into decline."

"At any rate, my performance was undeniably brilliant." Higuchi suddenly tooted his own horn. "It's the dawn of Japan!"

"How did you end up being Sakamoto Ryoma anyway?"

"Can't refuse a disciple's request."

"Now that's what makes the least sense of all," Jogasaki sighed. "Why are you the master? Why not me? Shouldn't I get more respect?"

In short, Jogasaki was frustrated by Akashi's lack of respect for him.

Listening to their fruitless exchange, I imagined a student life I might have had. If I had joined the Ablutions film club as a freshman instead of choosing the Keifuku Electric Railroad Research Society . . . I would surely have revolted against Boss Jogasaki's leadership. I have no doubt that I would have teamed up with Ozu to mass-produce trashy films, but since we're not as clever as Akashi, we'd have steadily lost our position in the club until, probably around autumn of our sophomore year, we'd have been met with the misery of exile. I could imagine the tragic end so vividly, it was as if I had already experienced it. So I couldn't help but sympathize strongly with Akashi.

Akashi, you keep running right down your own path!

People must run down the path they believe in. Compromises and subordination are worthless.

"This film is an absolute masterpiece," I said.

Jogasaki fell into a cranky silence, so we all awkwardly stopped talking.

It was still early, so Oasis was dead; besides us, there were only three other customers in the men's bath. Three men with towels wrapped tightly around their heads were sitting in a row along the wall shoulder-to-shoulder, showering with single-minded devotion. A bit of a weird bunch.

Eventually, Higuchi went to wash up, and Ozu eagerly

headed for the electric bath. This electric bath was known as the Killer Electric Bath thanks to its overly stimulating current; the fact that Ozu would voluntarily submit himself to such torture gives us a glimpse into his dark existence.

Just then we heard an amorous voice coming from the women's bath.

"Higuchiii! Jogasakiii!"

"Oh, is that Hanuki?" answered Higuchi. "I never see you here!"

"I thought I'd like to go take a bath for a change." Hanuki's easygoing voice echoed.

"Good idea. Such things give life some elegance."

I looked absentmindedly up at the ceiling.

Clouds of steam swirled around the rays of sun coming through the skylights.

At that moment, I was thinking of Akashi standing in the yard looking up at the sky after we finished filming. The view of her from behind was as divine as if she were enveloped in a heavenly glow.

Come to think of it, it's been nearly half a year since I met Akashi.

I first spoke to Akashi this past February, the day after Setsubun.

I remember that winter day so clearly: snowflakes fluttering down from the chilly, gray sky; Mount Hiei looking as though it had been dusted with sugar; Tadasu no Mori's riding grounds coated in white; Akashi striding toward me bundled up in a red scarf; and a little bear plushie buried in the snow.

The memories made me restless.

What have I been doing the past six months? While I'd been idling along, some Obstructor of Romance could have been training his hawk eyes on her. This was no time to be having a soak.

I stood up with a splash. "I'm going to go back ahead of you guys. I have an errand to run."

"Leaving so soon?" As I was getting out of the tub, Ozu, twitching in the electric bath, looked at me suspiciously and said, "You should relax, take your time."

• • •

When I left the bathhouse, the long twilight of August was just beginning.

I'm gonna do it! I'm gonna do it! I'm gonna do it!

I drummed on my bath bucket to psych myself up.

I had one goal: to ask Akashi out to see the Gozan Okuribi.

I knew of a secret place in the Mount Yoshida neighborhood where you could observe Mount Daimonji in comfort. I had discovered it on one of the pointless, solo rambles around town I took with the extra time on my hands after being exiled from the Keifuku Electric Railroad Research Society, and I decided that someday I would guide my crush there. You could say it was my lethal weapon in the game of love; if I didn't use it now, then when?

As I approached the Takano River, I saw a slender figure standing across the bridge on Mikage-dori. It was Akashi. She didn't seem to notice me and was walking toward Shimogamo

Shrine. Today the Kyoto Antiquarian Book Fair was being held in the forest at the shrine.

"After we're done cleaning up, I'm going to go to the book fair." That's what she had said when filming wrapped.

A flawless plan popped into my head.

Beneath a used bookstore tent, I would nonchalantly strike up a conversation with Akashi. If I let my eyes wander along the shelves as we chatted, I would surely be able to find any number of books about the Gozan Okuribi. Ever so nonchalantly, I would pick one up and flip through it in front of her. "Actually, the Gozan Okuribi are coming up, huh?" I would say. "They are," she would say. At that point, it would be nothing short of my duty as a gentleman to invite her to go see the five ceremonial bonfires.

"This is a once-in-a-lifetime chance!"

With a tremble of excitement, I rushed after Akashi into Tadasu no Mori.

Night had crept into the forest early. When I entered from the side, off the long approach to Shimogamo Shrine, a great many white tents were lining both sides of the riding grounds that stretched north to south. Shoppers had grown sparse, and a loudspeaker was announcing closing time. As if that voice was ushering her along, Akashi sped from tent to tent as light-footed as the deity Idaten.

To get to the point, I never did talk to her.

First, she was walking too quickly, so it would have been impossible to strike up a natural conversation.

Second, I couldn't bear to disturb her passionate book search.

Third, during the course of meandering between used bookstore tents, my senses returned to me.

Come to think of it, to Akashi, I was merely "Ozu's friend" or maybe "Higuchi's neighbor." Though I had done my best to support her in the production of *Lives of Bakumatsu Weaklings*, in the end, that was only one of her multitudinous works. Perhaps I was overvaluing my contribution. Perhaps the distance between us was not as small as I expected, and she still considered me a pebble by the wayside.

Let's say I invited her: "Would you like to go see the Gozan Okuribi with me?"

She might frown and say, "Why should I have to go with you?"

Just imagining that chilly tone made me shiver.

The more I thought, the heavier my steps grew. The distance between us was only widening; I didn't feel like I would ever catch up to her.

Eventually, my feet completely stopped, and I watched her speed away.

"I'll call it a day," I murmured, turning on my heel.

Before I knew it, I was out on the bank of the Kamo River.

I sat on a bench in the shade of an elm tree and watched the glittering of the water's surface for a time.

True, I was incapable of inviting Akashi out. But there would be no one more foolish than he who dared call my hesitation "spineless," for example, or "unmanly," or "wishy-washy," or any other superficial cookie-cutter insult. It was precisely because I respected Akashi as a human being that I hesitated to thrust my feelings upon her in a one-sided way, so this strategic retreat was no less than proof that I was a gentleman with an understanding of human nature's subtleties. A gentleman is well-versed in hesitation—even if it appears a bit like creepiness to an objective observer.

From the Kamo River's embankment, Mount Daimonji was visible.

"Wouldn't inviting her to see the Gozan Okuribi be too typical, anyway?"

For students who lived in Kyoto, there were any number of festivals to invite their sweethearts to: Aoi Matsuri, Gion Matsuri, the Gozan Okuribi, Kurama's Hi Matsuri, and so on. There was a time when I longed to invite someone special to an event like that. But relationships between men and women are relationships between individuals that must be built up carefully, according to each person's pace. They shouldn't be rushed recklessly ahead in order to conform to the year's event schedule.

If today's no good, there's always tomorrow.

If tomorrow's no good, there's always the next day.

If the next day's no good, there's always the day after that.

If I go back to Shimogamo Yusuiso, there's an air conditioner. Yes, indeed. Right now, I'm a man who has been given the wonderful environment known as a four-and-a-half-mat tatami room with an air conditioner. Everything starts now. A detailed plan, early nights and early mornings, tempering of the flesh, academic devotion. With that accumulation of fruitful days, I would become a man worthy of Akashi. Then we would surely grow closer in a natural way. Just as a vessel filled with water eventually overflows, what was supposed to happen, would.

I felt like I had seen the light.

"All right!" I shouted as I stood up, cradling my hope for tomorrow and my bath bucket to my chest.

But awaiting me when I returned to Shimogamo Yusu-iso from the Kamo River was a truly stupid turn of events. Nevertheless, that turn was not only my fate as an individual human, but also the trigger of a crisis that would affect the whole universe.

• • •

When I got back to Shimogamo Yusuiso, I heard animated voices coming from the second floor.

"Where'd he go?" Ozu's voice was loudest of all.

Apparently, Higuchi and those guys were still hanging out after our bath.

Upstairs, as I was walking down the hall, I saw that Higuchi and Ozu were lurking at the other end. Jogasaki and Hanuki were there, too. They were all peeking into the laundry-drying area, opening doors, and shoving aside junk in the hallway, looking for something. Just as I felt a worryingly cool breeze, I noticed that the door to 209 was wide open. They were using my air conditioner without asking again. Just as I was about to raise my voice in anger, Akashi appeared from the laundry-drying area. Apparently, while I was nursing my injured heart on the Kamo River, she had returned from the used book fair.

"Oh!" she gasped when she saw me.

"What? Is something wrong?" I asked.

At the sound of Akashi's voice, Higuchi, Ozu, Jogasaki,

and Hanuki turned to look at me. They were all ah-ing or oh-ing in surprise. Their eyes were all on my bath bucket, and they contained a reverence I'd never felt before.

"Aha, I see. So you're all set, huh?" said Hanuki. "I'm in love."

Even Jogasaki's face said he thought better of me. "You really know how to get the party started."

Anyway, I snatched the remote out of Jogasaki's hand and turned off 209's air conditioner. "Don't just go using my AC whenever you feel like," I said as I set the remote on the mini fridge, where there was also a half-drunk bottle of Coke.

Akashi looked concerned.

"Are you really going to go through with it?"

"Go through with what?"

"With what? The, uh . . . thing . . ."

"All right, all right. Let's see that dance now!" Ozu grabbed my arm and stood me in the middle of the hallway. The others either sat on the couch or pulled up a stool and gazed at me with anticipation. Standing there speechless with my bath bucket, I looked around at them. What did they think I was going to do?

"Dance? What dance?"

"Oh, c'mon, we were just talking about it." Ozu smirked as he screamed, "A naked dance!"

"A naked dance? Why would I do that?"

"Oh, you're going to feign dignity now?" Higuchi said, stroking his chin.

Jogasaki frowned. "Hey, it's lame to stall. If you're gonna do it, be a man and do it."

"We won't take our eyes off you," said Hanuki.

"No, I just have no idea what you're talking about." When I looked to Akashi in desperation, she was hiding behind Higuchi. Her complex, subtle expression was a combination of embarrassment, resignation, and intellectual curiosity.

"You already have your prop, don't you?" Ozu pointed at my bath bucket. "You can just use that to dance—like this!" He held an invisible bath bucket over his nether regions and demonstrated.

I can remember the way Ozu was dancing with that wicked smirk on his face in minute detail even now. He was truly the personification of evil. And in truth, it was via this devilish dance that Ozu not only demolished my future, but also put the entire universe at risk of destruction.

Ozu's right arm bumped the fridge, and that was when the Coke bottle tipped over. The dark, frothy liquid poured out and rapidly spilled off the top of the fridge.

Akashi screamed, "The remote!"

I shoved Ozu out of the way and ran over, but it was too late. Drenched in Coke, the remote lost all function.

● ● ●

With my soul having left my body an empty husk upon that tragedy, I said screw everyone's incomprehensible demands for a naked dance, and holed up in room 209. Then, after Akashi left, we held a wake for the air conditioner on Higuchi's request, as I previously explained.

Now we'll return the hands of time once again to the afternoon of August 12.

I was leaning against the wall in the hallway staring at Akashi's profile.

I wonder who she's going to see the Okuribi with.

With no regard for my worries, Akashi glared at her computer screen, pale-faced, her expression now quite intense. She must have been fretting over how to compile a film out of that footage. This probably wasn't a good time to ask her about her Okuribi date.

As I was brooding, she said, still gazing at the screen, "Hey, do you have a minute?" Her voice was tremendously serious.

Feeling like she must have read my mind, I froze in shock.

"Could you take a look at this scene? There's something bothering me."

Apparently she wanted advice about the movie. Relieved, I approached the couch and sat down next to her. Then I focused on the computer screen.

It was a shot of the landlady's garden and the kappa statue; the white-faced Iwakura Tomomi (that is, Ozu) and the sad-sack Shinsengumi were brawling. Iwakura Tomomi, twining himself around the kappa, was like a yokai; the Shinsengumi's fighting was utterly devoid of vigor; and on top of that, the apartment building's laundry-drying area was visible in the distance. As for what might bother a person about this video, it'd be quicker to list what wouldn't, but after watching the footage in silence for a little while, Akashi sharply said, "This."

"Where?"

"Here. Please direct your attention to the laundry-drying area." She paused the video and pointed at the screen.

There was a lanky figure standing in the laundry-drying area.

"That's Ozu, isn't it?" I said, before thinking, *Huh?* Then who was the one brawling in the foreground with the Shinsengumi? "There are two Ozus."

"I noticed when I was watching the footage just now," said Akashi. "Ozu doesn't have a twin, does he?"

"That's absurd! I've never heard anything about a twin."

"Maybe he's keeping him a secret from us or something,"

Hearing that from Akashi made me feel it might just be true. I was constantly in awe of Ozu's ability to get his fingers in everything. He was a member of the film club Ablutions, but also a disciple of Seitaro Higuchi. Yet that was only one facet of this strange man. He was involved in several other associations, and I heard that in some religious softball club as well as a certain shady campus organization, he was treated as an authority figure. How was it possible for this guy as weak-fleshed as me to be so superhumanly active? It couldn't all be explained away with the simple fact that he neglected his academics. Adopting Akashi's Multiple Ozu Theory would actually clear all of those questions up.

I examined the computer screen once more.

Ozu was leaning out from the apartment's laundry-drying area, watching himself cornered by the Shinsengumi, clinging to the kappa statue. The big smile on his face seemed to indicate he was supremely entertained. I could just hear his demonic laughter.

As I stared at that evil grin, the wriggling Ozu in my imagination went from one to two, from two to four, from four to eight, reproducing just like bacteria. It was as if he were a sickly-looking alien invading the planet.

Akashi and I looked at each other.

"What's going on?"

• • •

"Look at you two getting along so well!" A bright voice sounded from down the hall.

When I looked up, Hanuki and Jogasaki were walking over.

Akashi swiftly closed the video window and gave me a look. *She must be saying we should keep the terrible secret about Ozu to ourselves for a while.* I nodded. The Multiple Ozu Theory was extremely creepy, but getting to keep a secret with Akashi wasn't half bad.

Jogasaki gave a laconic greeting with his hands stuffed in his pockets, "Yo."

"Sure is hot out," said Hanuki. As I mentioned previously, Hanuki worked for a dentist as a hygienist and was friends with Jogasaki and Higuchi. "Is Higuchi here?"

"He just went with Ozu to the landlady's place," I said, standing up. "Though I imagine they'll be back soon."

"I was thinking the three of us could go for a meal. It's been so long. You know, we couldn't do it yesterday since Higuchi was all about the air conditioner wake. You two can come, too, if you want." Hanuki sat down next to Akashi. "So what ended up happening? How's the AC?"

"It's still busted, thank you very much," I said.

"My condolences. We still have a lot of summer left." She seemed more amused than sympathetic. Then she asked Akashi, "Are you going to be able to finish the film?"

"Yes, thank you," Akashi replied, petting her laptop.

"I'm looking forward to it. Higuchi played Sakamoto Ryoma, right?"

"He just repeated one line over and over!" Jogasaki complained. "Can you even call that acting?"

"You don't have to pay attention to this guy's opinions. He's got zero talent," Hanuki whispered in Akashi's ear. He may have had absolute authority in Ablutions, but Hanuki didn't care one bit about that.

Jogasaki was about to snark back when a bunch of junk collapsed loudly behind him. The junk in this hallway was always stacked in precarious ways, so things would fall if given the slightest opportunity.

Hanuki turned around and narrowed her eyes. "Hey, Jogasaki. What are you doing?"

"I didn't do anything!"

"You must have been touching something you shouldn't have been."

"What's with this apartment building? It's a total dump." Jogasaki grumbled under his breath as he began tidying up the junk with unexpected docility. Apparently when he was with Hanuki, his tyrannical tendencies softened.

"Aha!" Hanuki laughed before turning to me. "I wish I could have watched you guys film," she lamented.

Hearing that, I cocked my head. She had definitely been there at the end of the shoot. She had been swaggering around as usual, causing even more confusion on the already chaotic set.

"Weren't you on the set yesterday, Hanuki?"

"No? I had work until evening. Unlike you people, I devote myself to my labor."

"But you came to the bathhouse, didn't you?"

"The bathhouse?"

"You were shouting to us from the women's bath."

"Hold on. What are you talking about?"

"Weird. Jogasaki, you heard her, too, didn't you?"

"Yeah, I did. That was you, Hanuki!" Jogasaki replied from behind a mountain of junk, sounding put out.

"Are you sure the heat isn't getting to you? I just stopped by on my way home from work," she said in frustration. "Then the whole naked dance conversation started, Ozu spilled Coke on the remote, and that was it. I thought the whole thing was so bizarre."

For whatever reason, our stories weren't lining up. And it wasn't the first time in recent memory. It had happened the previous evening, after I came home from the used book fair. Everyone was in this hallway, and for some reason they were demanding that I dance naked. We all forgot about that once the Coke Incident happened, but we weren't on the same page then, either—to a spooky degree.

"Well, it's summer. No wonder you're out of it," Hanuki said with a yawn. "By the way, what are you doing over there, Jogasaki?"

"What do you guys suppose this is?"

Jogasaki was down the hall squatting, staring at some strange thing on the floor.

It was an old tatami mat, gleaming darkly as if it had been simmered for hours. And it wasn't just tatami. It seemed someone had ripped up one of the building's mats and altered it; a red seat for one had been attached, and in front of it there was even a control panel with a lever and various switches.

We gathered around Jogasaki.

"Hmm? I wonder."

"It was leaning up against this wall."

"It looks like a vehicle. But it doesn't have wheels."

"Maybe our master picked it up?"

"No, hold on. Ohhh, I see. So this goes like this." Jogasaki stood up a big lamp-like fixture that was attached to the contraption.

It couldn't have been just me. I had no doubt that all of us present recalled a certain nationally renowned masterpiece of manga. That round, blue cat robot had used a device like this to travel from the far-flung future. But it was such an obvious observation that I hesitated to voice it. No wonder we stood there in silence for a time.

Eventually Akashi spoke. "Maybe it's a time machine?"

Her quiet voice sounded embarrassed.

The wind chime by the laundry-drying area rang. It was summer.

• • •

We surrounded the time machine and laughed our heads off for a bit.

Whoever made it wasn't screwing around. The control panel had a spot to input years, months, and days, and if you spun the dials, the numbers changed as you would expect.

You could set it from −99 to +99 years. That is, to go ten years into the future, you would input "+10" and "August 12."

"I wonder who made it."

"Some tech wizard with too much time on their hands."

As we were bantering, Higuchi and Ozu came back from the landlady's place.

"Hullo, you seem to be having an awful lot of fun!" said Higuchi before holding out a hand to Jogasaki. "Hey, Jogasaki. I demand the return of my Vidal Sassoon."

Apparently Higuchi had tried calling Oasis, but they told him there was no shampoo in the lost and found. If Ozu or I hadn't stolen it, then Jogasaki had to be the culprit, was what Seitaro Higuchi's logic said—the bold deduction of someone bringing a tree trunk to a fistfight.

"If you want to apologize, now is the time, Jogasaki."

"Why would I know where your shampoo is?"

Then Hanuki interrupted. "Who cares about that? Higuchi, is this time machine yours?"

Higuchi looked down at the device on the hallway floor with interest. "Let's see. No, this doesn't belong to me."

"So then is it one of your pranks, Ozu?" asked Jogasaki, but Ozu shook his head.

"Ha, no. If I wanted to prank someone, I'd do something meaner."

True, it wasn't evil enough for someone like Ozu, who fueled himself on other people's misfortunes. Just leaving a "time machine" in the hallway didn't make anyone miserable. On the contrary, it only inspired warm laughter.

I peered at the control panel. It was set to −25 years,

August 12. Just for kicks, I set the years to 0 and the day to August 11. This way, the machine would go to yesterday. There didn't seem to be a way to set a time.

Suddenly, Higuchi gave Ozu a solemn order. "Depart, Ozu! On a voyage to the far reaches of time and space!"

"Understood, Master!"

Ozu shoved me out of the way and boarded the "time machine." Without a moment's delay, Hanuki, Akashi, and I took a step back and saluted him.

Ozu rested his hand on the lever and scanned our faces.

"Master, and everyone else, I'm grateful for your kindness these many months we've known one another. Though we may be separated across time and space, I, unworthy Ozu, will never forget the debt I owe you."

"Good. Be well, Ozu!" Higuchi nodded gravely.

With a theatrical flourish, Ozu pulled the lever.

"Goodbye! Take care of yourselves!"

In the next instant, Ozu warped before our eyes. No, I suppose I should say that the space containing him warped as a whole. Then a glaring flash filled the hallway, and a whirlwind blew in fierce spirals. I shielded my head instinctively. After I was battered by the wind with no idea what was happening, the whirling abruptly stopped, and the area fell silent. In the eerie quiet, the only sound was the ringing of the wind chime.

When I cautiously opened my eyes, I saw that Ozu and the "time machine" had vanished.

"What was that just now?" said Hanuki.

"Where did Ozu go?" said Akashi.

We all looked at one another. Everyone was stunned.

We searched in the laundry-drying area, behind the junk, in the storeroom, in Higuchi's room and mine, on the stairs leading to the first floor, and even in the bathroom, but Ozu was nowhere to be found. There was no way he could have hidden himself and the time machine so fast in the first place.

"Maybe it was real . . . ?" Akashi murmured.

Jogasaki snapped back in irritation, "No way."

"Then where did he go?" I said. "There's nowhere for him to hide!"

"There must be some kind of trick to it. It has to be one of Ozu's schemes."

Higuchi and Hanuki sat together on the couch. Apparently they had given up on thinking, having reached the opinion that "what will be will be." That was actually the correct attitude. A bit later, the same flash of light filled the hallway, and Ozu and the "time machine" returned in a swirling whirlwind.

"My word," he said, looking around at us. "This is serious, everyone."

"Where were you?" I asked.

"Yesterday," Ozu answered nonchalantly. "When I pulled the lever, everything around me went *smyoosh*. Before I knew it, the hallway was empty; you were all gone. With no clue what was going on, I went out to the laundry-drying area, where I heard excited voices coming from the landlady's house. When I leaned over the railing to take a look, I saw a movie being filmed. It was *Lives of Bakumatsu Weaklings*. I thought, *Wow, this is amazing*, and stayed to observe for a bit, but then I thought I had better report back, so here I am. This thing is quite the device."

"Oh, come the fuck on." It was no surprise that Jogasaki would be angry. There's a limit to how preposterous a tale you can tell.

"Ah!" Akashi gasped just then. "The video!"

"Video?" I asked.

"The Multiple Ozu Theory!"

The creepy video I had seen just earlier instantly came to mind.

Akashi sat on the floor and opened her computer, and we all peered into the screen: Iwakura Tomomi clinging to the kappa statue, the wonkadonk Shinsengumi crowding around him—and, visible in the laundry-drying area, the second Ozu.

"Oh, that's me. The me playing Iwakura Tomomi rampaging in the foreground is yesterday-me, and the one observing from the laundry-drying area is today-me. See? Just like I said."

"So there were two of you yesterday?" asked Hanuki.

Akashi murmured, "So that means . . . ," and I looked at the "time machine": a world-shaking new invention that had appeared out of nowhere in a student apartment building . . .

As everyone was holding their breath, Seitaro Higuchi slowly rose from the couch and solemnly intoned, "It means this is a real time machine."

• • •

In the hundred-plus years since the great British author H. G. Wells published his novel *The Time Machine*, the idea of a machine that travels through time has been used over and over.

Why do time machines appeal to our hearts so? Because time is the most fundamental puzzle to mankind, as well as a universal restraint that no one can escape. Everyone's day has only twenty-four hours, and you can kick and scream all you like, but the sand in the hourglass will fall without end; a summer once passed will never come again. That's why we dream over and over of a machine for traveling through time. Transcending time is nothing short of a revolt against the fundamental human condition, a godly power, and the ultimate freedom.

Why would such an amazing device show up here of all places?

Hanuki let out a low whistle. "So, Ozu, that means you're a time traveler."

According to grimy Time Traveler Ozu, traveling through time took but an instant. When he pulled the lever and closed his eyes, it took only the time to open them again for it to be yesterday.

Akashi got into the time machine and stared at the control panel.

"Ozu, what time yesterday did you arrive?"

"It was right before I knocked over the kappa statue, so . . ."

It was currently two thirty p.m., and he had knocked over the kappa statue the previous day at about the same time.

"So that must mean you travel to the same time of day?" Akashi murmured. "Well, yeah, there aren't hour or minute dials."

I crouched down next to Akashi and looked at the control panel. Since the year scale went to 99, the furthest you could go in one trip would be the Taisho period, but if you traveled again from where you landed, you could go further back in time, like a skipping stone. And the same went for the future. When I looked at Akashi beside me, her eyes were twinkling with excitement.

"That guy from before must have made it."

"Guy from before?"

"You know, that kinda dorky guy."

I recalled the dorky fellow who had shown up to talk to us earlier.

No matter how generous you were, he had just seemed like a freshman, lovable despite having failed every step of the way in attaining a new look for his college debut. But they say a clever hawk hides its talons. That unfashionable dorkiness could have been the disguise of an unparalleled genius.

Just then, the sound of someone padding down the hall approached.

I was sure the owner of the time machine was making an appearance, but then an ear-splitting voice rang out, "Oh-ho! The gang's all here!" It was Jogasaki's right-hand man in the film club Ablutions, the one who played the role of Susumu Ginga in *Lives of Bakumatsu Weaklings*: Aijima.

"Jogasaki, what's the party about?"

"It's not really a party," Jogasaki said dubiously. "How about you? What are you doing here?"

"I made an appointment with this guy here yesterday." Aijima pointed at me. "Did you find the glasses?"

"Glasses?"

"Yeah, my glasses."

But Aijima was already wearing glasses. When I pointed that out, he said, "But I explained this yesterday . . ." in exasperation. "These are the ones for my costume. My usual glasses, I lost here yesterday. You said you would look for them for me."

Once again we were out of sync; it was the exact same weirdness I'd already experienced.

"I can't count on you for anything." Aijima emitted a stream of gripes until the moment he laid eyes on the time machine. "Ah!" he gasped. "This! It's this thing!"

"You've seen it before, Aijima?" Akashi asked, and he ran over to it.

"It was here yesterday. I thought for sure it was a hallucination, but look, here it is. It's a time machine, right?"

"Yes, that's right. It's a time machine."

"It's really so well done. Who made it?"

Apparently he thought it was a movie prop.

When Akashi told him that no, it was an actual time machine, he was shocked for a moment. Then he said, "Wait, are you guys pranking me?"

"No, it's nothing like that. This is a real time machine."

"Because I hate it when people gang up on someone to trick them."

We explained about Ozu's time traveling and showed Aijima the video that proved it. But he only narrowed his eyes behind his glasses and sneered. Well, that was no surprise. The one who had used the machine was Ozu, the least trustworthy man in the world, and you could edit a video as much as you wanted after the fact.

"Why don't we try it again?" Akashi asked. "Then you'll believe us, right, Aijima?"

"Well, if I saw it with my own eyes, I might change my mind," he said, but he was still sneering.

• • •

"All right, fellows. When to?" said Seitaro Higuchi.

Akashi was the first to put her hand up.

"Why don't we go see the future? Like maybe ten years or so forward in time."

The ability to see the future before anyone else—surely that's the real fun of a time machine. But there was one big problem. If we went to go see the world of ten years from now, there was no guarantee anything good would be waiting for us.

"It would suck if you were dead or something," said Hanuki.

If I found out about a future like that, I would inevitably lose my will to go on. Unable to focus on my studies, I would redo a year and eventually drop out. Frightened of the impending time limit, I would hole up in my room overindulging in food and drink; the debauched lifestyle and mental stress would result in ruined health, so that by ten years down the line I'd drop dead. It could very well be a self-fulfilling prophecy.

"Yeah, the future's too risky, Akashi."

"I see what you mean."

"Life would be boring if you knew what was going to happen next," said Higuchi. "The future should be forged with your own hands."

The second suggestion was Ozu's: "Let's go to the Jurassic period and play with the dinosaurs." But the Jurassic period was 150 million years ago, and our time machine could only go back in increments of ninety-nine years. To go back that far, we'd have to jump about 1.5 million times. So even if we were operating the machine 24-7, we would be dead quite a while before we reached the Jurassic period.

The third suggestion was mine: spring, two years ago. I thought I could secretly support my freshman self and guide him toward a rose-colored campus life. The most important thing was to prevent him from meeting Ozu. But Ozu saw through my plan and said, "Then I'll go with you and turn your freshman self into even more of a wreck." The time-transcending feud between Ozu and me was unanimously rejected.

It was a lot harder than expected to decide where to go with the time machine.

"Then how about sometime benign, like the Edo period?" said Hanuki. "Wouldn't you like to see a samurai?"

"That's an idea," I said. "And it would only take two jumps to get there."

"If we're going to do that, how about we go to the end of the Tokugawa shogunate?" said Higuchi.

There were immediately voices in agreement. It was actually a splendid idea.

In Kyoto during the Bakumatsu period, the real Sakamoto Ryoma and Saigo Takamori, the Shinsengumi, and so on were prowling around in the alleys—exactly the setting of *Lives of*

Bakumatsu Weaklings. If we took a camera with us, we'd be able to film as much of Bakumatsu-era Kyoto as we wanted, collecting footage that all the money in the world couldn't buy.

"Can I go get a camera first?" asked Akashi, her eyes gleaming.

It was Jogasaki who hit her with a cold bucket of water.

"Aren't any of you the slightest bit concerned?"

"What, Jogasaki? It's not like you're going to go, are you?" said Hanuki.

"Why would I?" he spat in response. "Even if I give you the benefit of my giant doubt and the time machine turns out to be real, that doesn't mean it'll keep working properly. What'll you do if it breaks down where you end up? You gonna just keep living in the Bakumatsu?"

"We'll cross that bridge when we come to it," said Higuchi in his easygoing way. "Humans can survive in any age."

Certainly a tengu-like being such as Higuchi might be able to baffle the Shinsengumi and lordless samurai and make it through the chaos of the Bakumatsu. But would the rest of us, 100 percent children of now with such meager life forces, be able to survive? Everyone except Higuchi exchanged glances.

"Guess we should give up on that idea?" whispered Hanuki.

After a brief silence, Akashi spoke up.

"Why don't we try somewhere nearby?"

"Let's just do yesterday for now," I said.

"Yeah, if something happens, we'll be able to get back on our own."

The trip had been scaled down quite a lot, but a journey of a thousand miles begins with a single step.

In the present, the time was just after two thirty p.m. Mapped to yesterday, that meant we were still filming at the landlady's house. We had wrapped things up and left around three thirty, so this building would be empty. We went to the bathhouse Oasis a little after four, and I had returned to the apartment building after my strategic retreat from the used book fair after six, and that was when the Coke Incident happened . . .

Having thought that far, I experienced a divine revelation.

"Hey, I just had an awesome idea!"

In yesterday's now, the air conditioner remote wasn't broken yet. So if we took the time machine to yesterday and brought back the remote from before it was broken, wouldn't we be able to use room 209's AC again?

What better use for a time machine could there be?

"Ahh," Higuchi moaned. "I didn't think of that."

"That's a clever use for a time machine. Great idea!" said Akashi.

The only question was who would go. We attempted to all get on at once, but staying in such athletic positions required the skills of a troupe of Chinese acrobats; if we weren't careful, someone could get thrown off mid-time-slip. We decided to send three people to yesterday, and the members would be decided by playing Rock Paper Scissors.

The resulting first exploratory squad consisted of Higuchi, Hanuki, and Ozu.

Akashi looked sadly at the scissors she had thrown. "I'm no good at Rock Paper Scissors."

"Ozu, you already went once, so why don't you give your spot to Akashi?"

"No way. After all, I'm the world's only time traveler, the pilot of this machine. You could say I'm indispensable."

"We're just going to take a peek and come straight back," said Hanuki, to console Akashi.

"Please don't worry about me," said Akashi. "Bon voyage, everyone."

With that, the first exploratory squad (Higuchi, Hanuki, and Ozu) boarded the time machine.

Ozu sat in the driver's seat and set the date before looking us over.

"Well then, everyone, we're off."

"Come back as soon as you have the remote," I insisted. "In about thirty minutes, our yesterday selves will be back, you know."

"I've caused you so much trouble. What happened with the air conditioner was a deeply regrettable error. But now we have a time machine. I'll bring the remote back if it's the last thing I do. Until then, I wish you well."

"Whatever, just hurry up."

When Ozu said, "All right," and pulled the lever, there was a flash followed by a whirlwind. The time machine carrying the three of them disappeared, and only the rest of us remained.

The only sound was the ringing of the wind chime.

So it was that the first exploratory squad set out on their voyage to yesterday. But from the moment we saw them off, an anxiety difficult to describe sprouted in my breast: *Were they really the right people for the job?*

Seitaro Higuchi, Ozu, and Hanuki—reflecting on it now, those were the worst three people we could have picked.

• • •

The wind chime stopped ringing, and the area fell silent.

With Ozu and the others having vanished with the time machine, the building of four-and-a-half-mat tatami rooms remained as it had been. It felt as if all the oppressive afternoon heat hit at once.

In a quivering voice, Aijima said, "Jogasaki, what's going on?"

"Seems like that time machine's the real deal."

"No way. This isn't some sci-fi movie . . ."

"Aijima," Akashi called to him as he stumbled in disbelief. "Won't it be dangerous for you to be standing there when the time machine returns?"

He yelped, "Eep!" and jumped aside.

We encircled the projected arrival point of the time machine. There was no way I was getting fused with Ozu like in some horror movie to become a yokai-Ozu-human.

Higuchi, Hanuki, and Ozu had vanished from the world of today and were in the world of yesterday. That meant that yesterday, there were two of each of them.

"This is kind of weird," murmured Akashi. "They used the time machine today, so they're in yesterday. But yesterday, before we even found the time machine, they were already there, then, right?"

"It's confusing."

"It is."

"What's the deal with the time machine, anyway?" said Aijima. "How'd a thing like that end up here?"

"How would we know?" I said.

"You don't know? You don't know?!" he shouted, incredulous. "Yet you're riding it around anyway?"

"That's what I've been saying!" said Jogasaki in exasperation.

That's when it happened.

"Umm, excuse me." Someone hesitantly called to us from down the hall.

When we all closed our mouths and turned to look, the guy seemed overwhelmed. Mushroom-cap hair, a simple outfit of a white T-shirt tucked neatly into pants—it was the same dork from earlier.

Aijima replied with an air of recognition. "What, you again?"

"Do you know him?" Akashi asked in surprise, but then Aijima looked even more surprised than she did.

"Didn't he introduce himself when we met him yesterday?"

"Huh?"

"Ozu's cousin, right?"

Needless to say, we were flabbergasted.

We hadn't heard anything about this from Ozu.

"You're here to check out the campus over summer vacation, right?" asked Aijima, but Dorky recoiled, seemingly creeped out.

"No, that's not me . . . "

"What?"

"Wrong person."

"Hold up, that can't be right. We talked for so long yesterday."

"I've never met you before. And I'm not this Ozu person's cousin." Then Dorky said something that was impossible to ignore. "I mean, the time period doesn't even match up."

The time period doesn't even match up. The implications of that statement were clear.

Akashi shoved Aijima aside and said, "What's that supposed to mean?"

Dorky replied with a suggestive smile. "Everyone, I'd like you to listen calmly to what I have to say . . ." Then he abruptly stopped talking. "Oh?" he murmured apprehensively and rushed over to the pile of junk in the hallway. "Sorry, but wasn't there some kind of strange machine here? About the size of a tatami mat, with a lever and a control panel and stuff . . ."

"You mean the time machine?" I said, and his eyes went wide.

"So you have seen it!"

"Seen it? Well, I suppose you could say that."

Dorky smiled cheerfully. "So the truth is, I came here using that—from exactly twenty-five years in the future!"

• • •

Dorky politely introduced himself. "My name is Tamura."

The reason he had such a baby face and comported himself so innocently was that he was a college freshman—a college freshman twenty-five years from now. Not only that, but he was a resident of Shimogamo Yusuiso; he said he had been living in room 209, same as me. I was glad to hear that this building, which in the present might already be taken for abandoned, still existed a quarter century in the future, but it was also hard to believe.

"Are time machines totally normal in your time?" I asked, and Tamura puffed out his chest proudly.

"No, no. We made it ourselves."

"Who's we?"

"Everyone at Shimogamo Yusuiso."

It happened in May, twenty-five years from now.

The landlady (still alive and well) summoned all the residents of Shimogamo Yusuiso to do a major clean of the storage room on the second floor. Afterward, as they celebrated being finished with the cans of beer that were their pay, a physics grad student began expounding on whether time machines were possible or not.

He was a man who had nearly been ousted from his lab for the eccentric theories he was always spouting, but he declared that it was possible to build a time machine. It wasn't the kind of thing you could go believing willy-nilly, but as the debate wore on, excitement grew, and finally they said, "If that's true, then let's build one."

The students spent their precious summertime busily collecting parts; instead of visiting home as they were meant to, they assembled a time machine bit by bit under the instruction of this grad student. The member who dropped out because he chose love over friendship, the financial trouble regarding machine parts, the landlady's demands for rent, the role played by a visiting foreign scholar to the graduate school of engineering, and other episodes are tangential to the main thread, so I'll omit them here.

Three months later, on August 12, the time machine—a crystallization of their sweat and tears—was complete. And the one chosen as its first pilot was Tamura.

"No one wanted to go first. And I was a freshman, so . . ."

"So you're basically like that dog Laika, who got put in the spaceship."

"Right, exactly."

Tamura didn't seem very concerned about being experimented on.

And that's how Tamura, mankind's first time machine pilot, arrived precisely twenty-five years earlier on August 12—that is, ten a.m. this morning at our apartment building.

It had been quiet. No wonder; it was the morning after the wake for the air conditioner. Everyone left in the building was sleeping like filthy logs. "I knocked and knocked, but no one answered," said Tamura. Now that he mentioned it, though, I did feel as though I had heard some knocking while I was still half-asleep.

"Sorry about that."

"I thought there would be more of a welcome. But since I had nothing better to do, I went outside to explore. I was interested in seeing Kyoto of twenty-five years ago, you know. It was just after I got back from wandering around that I ran into you."

"Why'd you run off like that before?" Akashi asked, and Tamura winced and scratched his head awkwardly.

"I was just so surprised to see my master."

"Your master? You mean Higuchi?"

"I thought maybe he had ridden the time machine with me. He's at Shimogamo Yusuiso twenty-five years in the future, too—oh, I wonder if it's okay for me to tell you that."

"He's still here in twenty-five years?" said Jogasaki, before murmuring, "Unbelievable."

According to Tamura, Seitaro Higuchi still lived in Shimogamo Yusuiso room 210 a quarter of a century later, whispered about as the "Guardian Deity of Four-and-a-Half-Mat Tatami Rooms" as well as a "tengu who crashed into a four-and-a-half-mat tatami room by accident," and treated with the respect due the greatest perpetual student in the building. In other words, not a thing had changed.

"I thought he was just repeating a grade, so I never expected to see him in this time period. I never heard a word about it from him."

"Still, you didn't have to run away."

"I was just so surprised that I panicked, ah-ha-ha." Tamura laughed merrily. "I may not look like it, but I'm easily upset."

"Should we keep this a secret from Master Higuchi?" asked Akashi, and I hmm'd in response.

If Seitaro Higuchi learned that his fate was to still be living here after a quarter century, he seemed likely to stroke his chin and say, "Nothing wrong with that." That said, telling him his future when he hadn't asked struck me as unnecessary. We agreed to keep it a secret.

"So where is our master?" asked Tamura.

"Ah, he just stepped out briefly, to yesterday," I said.

"He's using the time machine," said Akashi. "Sorry, we didn't know it was yours."

"Ohhh, I see. So that's where it went," Tamura said.

"Apologies for using it without permission."

"No, that's perfectly all right."

"But won't everyone worry if you don't go back soon?"

"I'm fine. After all, it's a time machine. I can just go back to the time right after I left. Then no time will have even passed for them."

"Does that time machine have hour and minute settings?" I asked. We didn't see a dial for that.

"Does it not?" Tamura asked, surprised.

"There were only years, months, and days."

"Ack, I didn't realize." He stood there blankly for a moment but regained composure right away. "Well, not much we can do about that then, is there?"

"You're really winging it, huh?"

"I may not look like it, but yeah, I tend to." Tamura laughed. "Ah-ha-ha! Anyway, I'll just wait here."

The dorky guy from the future sat himself on the couch.

• • •

For a time, it was silent. Cicada cries were audible in the distance.

After a while, Tamura murmured, "It's so hot," and wiped away his sweat with a scroll-patterned hand towel. There wasn't much futuristic about him at all. I think we all felt the same way, but Aijima didn't even try to hide his suspicion.

"You're so dorky."

"Oh?"

"You don't look like you're from the future. I just don't see it."

"And yet, here I am, a man from the future!"

It wasn't only his clothes—even the way he talked felt retro.

Gazing at this unfuturistic man from the future, I imagined what the world twenty-five years from now must be like. What kind of life would I be leading? If still alive, I would be in my midforties. I'd probably have a wife and kids; I'd have accumulated a decent amount of life experience and would probably be performing well in a diverse array of settings as a socially capable individual. That was all well and good; the issue was that I couldn't see how that would be an extension of my current four-and-a-half-mat tatami room lifestyle. It goes without saying that Ozu was the one responsible for everything.

Akashi asked Tamura, "What's Kyoto like in the future?"

"Hmm. It's not that different. There's a used book fair at Shimogamo Shrine; the Kamo River and Mount Hiei are still there. It's almost time for the Gozan Okuribi. That's how it is in our time, too."

"Well, it is Kyoto, after all," I said.

"Oh, but there is one thing I found moving. There's a bathhouse called Oasis across the Takano River, right? In our time, there's a convenience store where it stood. I was happy to get to see the original when I went out exploring. Like, 'So this is where my dad used to take his baths . . .'"

"Your father spent time in Kyoto, too?"

"That's right." Tamura leaned in. "Not only that, but exactly around this time."

Apparently the reason Tamura ended up living at Shimogamo Yusuiso was that his dad had decided, without even consulting with him on the day they were getting him enrolled in school. A whole other quarter of a century had passed since now, so you can guess how run-down and abandoned it looked. Apparently, when Tamura was hesitating at the entrance to the building, his father had murmured, "Spare the four-and-a-half-mat tatami room and spoil the child." I must say, Tamura's pops had some backbone.

I tried to recall the names on the shoe cubbies, but Tamura wasn't in my memories.

"Maybe he lives in a different building," said Tamura. "At any rate, since this is twenty-five years ago, my mom and dad are around this neighborhood somewhere."

"Wait," said Akashi. "Your mother's here, too?"

"Supposedly my mom and dad met during their student days. But they lie so much, I have no idea if it's true. That's why when I got in the time machine, I picked this era to return to. I want to know the truth behind how they met."

"That's interesting. Why don't we go look for them?"

"Sounds fun!"

The one who dampened our enthusiasm was once again Jogasaki.

"Don't. If they see this dorky kid and stop feeling like having him, then what?"

"What a horrible thing to say!" Tamura was understandably miffed. "They're my mom and dad. They would never think that!"

"Except you're not born yet, right? Your parents are still college students; they're not ready for anything. If you're a time traveler, you should be way more concerned. If you accidentally ruin your parents' relationship, you could disappear!"

"Disappear? How?"

"Changing the present will change the future. That much should be obvious."

At that point Jogasaki seemed to be seized by a grave apprehension. Glaring into space, he murmured, "Wait." Seeing the look on his face made a bad feeling flood my breast.

Suddenly Akashi gasped, "That remote."

That was the bad feeling's true form.

Change the present, and the future changes. So if you change the past, the present changes.

"Ozu and crew went to yesterday in the time machine, right?" said Jogasaki, thinking aloud. "If they obtain yesterday's remote, then it will never have broken. The past will change. So then what happens to us right now?"

What *would* happen to us?

If Coke didn't spill on the remote yesterday, we wouldn't hold the wake for the air conditioner, and Akashi wouldn't take the remote to the electronics store. Everything after the Coke Incident would change. In other words, the today that existed as the result of the Coke ruining the remote would cease to exist—along with us living in it.

"The us of right now will disappear," I said.

"You can't say that now!" Jogasaki grabbed my collar. "This was your idea! Take responsibility!"

"Sure, but how?"

"Hold on. This might not end with us disappearing." Jogasaki thrust me away and murmured something horrible. "Let's say Ozu and them come back with the remote. It's hard to know how that will change the flow of time—anything could happen. Just as an example, it's possible that a chain reaction of little changes triggered by taking the remote could cause yesterday-Ozu to die in an accident. Then Ozu would have died yesterday, so he wouldn't be able to ride the time machine back to yesterday today. That's a serious paradox. If Ozu can't go back to yesterday, then he wouldn't have died yesterday!"

Akashi furrowed her brow and said, "That is indeed a paradox. It goes against the laws of the universe."

Finally, I understood what Jogasaki was getting at.

• • •

I'd like you to recall the film *Lives of Bakumatsu Weaklings*.

The alteration of time that occurs when college student Susumu Ginga slips from a twenty-first-century, four-and-a-half-mat tatami room to the latter days of the Tokugawa shogunate leads to a massive catastrophe—the disappearance of the universe.

At first glance, it seems like a hacky plot point, but it was the logical outcome of our debate on the subject.

Let's say Susumu Ginga prevented the Meiji Restoration from occurring. In that case, he never would have time-slipped due to an accident while experimenting, which contradicts the whole premise "Susumu Ginga prevented the Meiji Restoration." If we think in terms of proof by contradiction, then the sensible conclusion would be that it's impossible to create a time machine, because it would cause time paradoxes. But for this movie, our premise was that time machines were possible. The story couldn't even start if they weren't.

So then how could we resolve the paradoxes caused by the time machine?

Akashi and I had hotly debated this question. Omitting the details, this was our conclusion:

(i)   Time machines exist.
(ii) But time machines cause a fundamental paradox.
(iii) So this universe where time machines exist is all wrong.

The tragic end of *Lives of Bakumatsu Weaklings*, in which the universe vanishes, was where that conclusion led us. No matter how correct it was logically, I couldn't help but feel that it might not make for a very good movie, which is why I asked Akashi over and over again whether she was really sure she wanted to film it that way.

The film scenario bore a horrifying resemblance to our current predicament.

Certainly the Meiji Restoration and an air conditioner remote are on a different scale. But in the sense that they can cause a serious paradox, they're exactly the same.

That meant we were on the brink of universal destruction.

• • •

Jogasaki's face was white as a sheet. "That's why I said we shouldn't do it."

"Why are you all getting so freaked out?" said Aijima. "The time machine has gotta be a fake, right?"

"That's enough out of you. Shut it!"

Aijima shrank from Jogasaki's threatening tone.

"Seems like a bit of a mess," said Tamura.

It pissed me off that he said that as though it had nothing to do with him. "How can you be so nonchalant?"

When I reproached him, he sounded confused. "But I'm not from this time." He had zero awareness that he was the ringleader in all this space-time trouble. One could only conclude that he fundamentally lacked a logical view of the space-time continuum.

"I just came to visit this time on my machine. You're the ones who used it without permission. Yet it's still my fault?" he said.

I didn't say anything back.

I had had that whole debate with Akashi, but when faced with a real time machine, I didn't have any apprehension whatsoever. I can only say that my eyes were clouded with self-interest. I plunged the entire universe into a crisis for a single AC remote. The one lacking a logical view of the time-space continuum wasn't Tamura; it was none other than me.

"It's too soon to give up," Akashi said levelheadedly. "When they come back with the remote, let's go return it right away. The Coke spilled after everyone got back from the bathhouse, right? I'm pretty sure that was just after six p.m. If we return it before then without anyone realizing, everything should line up."

But Ozu and crew still weren't back; second by second, time receded into the past.

It was so quiet that it seemed like we were all anticipating ruin. In the silence, I started to feel as though the reality surrounding me was as fragile as glass. The muggy heat of the apartment, the ringing of the wind chime, the more distant cries of the cicadas—it all started to lose reality.

When I looked at Akashi, she was sitting up straight, staring intently at the projected arrival point of the time machine. I still couldn't see a single drop of sweat on her face in profile. If the universe vanished, would this unusual person disappear, too?

I said her name without thinking: "Akashi."

The moment she started to turn around, a noise like a lightning strike reverberated.

Finally, Ozu and the others were back. That's what we thought. But when we ran toward the machine, our jaws dropped in shock. The time machine was empty.

Akashi murmured, "How? What happened over there?"

When we peered into the seat, we found a piece of paper stuck to it. Written with a hand as shady as that of a tengu's apology was the following line:

You guys should come, too.
Seitaro Higuchi

TWO

August 11

Late the previous fall, I'd had a bizarre dream.

Deeply hurt by internal conflict in the Keifuku Electric Railroad Research Society, I had severed all my ties to the world and holed up in my four-and-a-half-mat tatami room.

The dream went like this: After a long sleep, I wake up in my bed. The usual ceiling, the usual four-and-a-half-mat tatami room, the usual quiet. And yet a strange disquiet in my breast. When I open the door to go to the communal bathroom, I find not the apartment building's hallway, but a mirror image of my room. And through that room's window is another one. No matter how far I go, it's all four-and-a-half-mat tatami rooms. At some point, I had become trapped in a curious world of tatami.

Though it made no sense at all, it was a bizarrely realistic dream.

During summer vacation, I kept recalling that weird dream—because the barren days going by one after the other seemed to me to be a lot like the countless four-and-a-half-mat tatami rooms. Today, same as yesterday; tomorrow, same as today—a grand matrix of four-and-a-half-mat tatami rooms, none better than the last, extending to the far reaches of space-time. If yesterday were the same as today, and tomorrow and today were also the same, then how could this summer ever end?

I'm wandering an endless summertime . . .

• • •

When Akashi and I rode the time machine to yesterday, it was hard to tell at a glance upon arrival whether it was really yesterday. Sweltering afternoon heat, junk piled up in the hallway, the sound of the wind chime swaying in the breeze . . . Could there possibly be a time trip that made it harder to tell any difference than this?

But on Higuchi's door, 210, was a notice that said, "Acting in a film at the landlady's house." Higuchi didn't have a phone, so for the convenience of friends and disciples who visited, he always left a note with the reason when he went out. That meant that at this very moment, we were filming *Lives of Bakumatsu Weaklings*.

"Akashi, this really does seem to be yesterday."

When I turned around, Akashi was crouching down in a feeble little ball.

"Sorry, I'm feeling a bit sick . . ."

True, you would be hard pressed to call the time machine a pleasant ride. The moment we crossed time made me dizzy, and I hated the feeling of my guts being jostled around. But I was fine, so time travel must really not agree with Akashi.

She took my hand to stand up and collapsed onto the couch in the hallway.

"You . . . have to get the remote . . ."

Just a little while ago—of course, it was "tomorrow," but in any case, when the empty time machine came back—there had been only one course of action for those of us facing the disappearance of the universe. We had to go to yesterday, make sure the remote broke as it was meant to, and promptly take Ozu and the others back.

Jogasaki just said, "Fix it!" and didn't make any move to board the machine, and Aijima simply scoffed. Tamura said, "I'll go, too!" but I respectfully declined his offer; it would only have made things more complicated.

Akashi and I have the fate of the entire universe on our shoulders.

It was just after three p.m., almost the time that filming of *Lives of Bakumatsu Weaklings* would wrap. The crew would be back here in no time.

"Where is it? Where is it? Where is it?" I looked all over my room and the hallway, but I couldn't find the remote anywhere.

There was only one possible reason for that: Ozu.

"We need to find him," said Akashi.

"No, you should rest, Akashi."

"I can't do that. Everyone will be back soon—" She sat up and—*ulp*—vomited again, bringing tears to her eyes.

I carried the time machine to the laundry-drying area and covered it with a sheet I found hanging there. As I busied myself with camouflaging, I could hear the students' animated voices from the landlady's house. The film club was breaking down the set.

When I turned to head back from the laundry-drying area, someone was walking down the hall toward me. The person, dressed as Saigo Takamori, gave us a dubious look.

"Huh? You guys are already back?"

It was Jogasaki (from yesterday).

Akashi slowly sat up on the couch.

Considering that any move we made could influence the flow of time and plunge the universe into crisis, we couldn't say anything careless. We both clammed up and froze.

Jogasaki's look grew even more suspicious.

"What's up? You guys are acting weird."

"Not a single thing about us is weird," I said. "We're extremely normal."

Perhaps wanting to hurry up and fling off his hot costume, Jogasaki shook his head with a "Well, whatever," and went to go into room 209. But the moment he stepped inside, the sweaty, fake Saigo Takamori shouted, "What the hell?!" and recoiled. "Hey, gimme the remote!"

"If you're looking for the remote, it must be in there," I said.

"It's not."

"What are you talking about? It can't not be in there."

"If it were in there, I wouldn't be telling you it wasn't, would I? Are you saying I gotta change in this sauna?"

Irritated as he pulled out the towels that had been stuffed under his kimono, he came toward me and said, "Give me the remote."

He had some nerve getting that high-handed. But the remote was gone. As I was elusively making excuses, Jogasaki seemed to find my attitude suspicious again. "There's definitely something weird going on," he said. "What are you doing here? They're still breaking down the set out there, aren't they?"

"We just had something we needed to do. We'll be right back."

"And when did you guys change?"

"We didn't change."

"Um, yes, you did."

"You're imagining things. You must be tired from filming."

"No, my eyes don't play tricks. You definitely changed clothes."

Suddenly, Akashi stood up and angrily said, "Why are you getting all up in our faces?" The color had finally returned to her cheeks. "As a human being, I'm free to be here or there, to change or not, as I please. Why should I have to report every little thing I do to you? Just because you're a senior member of the club doesn't give you the right to manage my personal life. I protest this flagrant violation of my privacy!"

"H-h-h-hold on a sec!" Jogasaki revealed his natural inability to take criticism. "I'm not trying to violate your privacy, Akashi!"

"Then could you leave us alone?"

"I just want the AC remote . . ."

"You have it. I've been telling you this."

"No, but . . . the . . . okay." Jogasaki shrank and fell silent.

Then Aijima (from yesterday) came over, saying, "Nice work today, everybody." But when he saw me and Akashi, he let out a dopey yelp, "Huh?! When did you two get back? I thought you were still breaking down the set."

If we dillydallied here much longer, our selves (from yesterday) would be back. We needed to get through this even if we had to send Jogasaki and Aijima scattering. Just as I had steeled my resolve, a "Yeahhhhhhhh!!!" like that of a legendary rock star echoed throughout the hallway.

Whirling around in shock, we found Hanuki standing there with her hands on her hips.

She thrust her hands into the air and shouted, "Time machines are the best!"

• • •

With no regard for how pale Akashi and I had gone, Hanuki frolicked our way. I could practically hear the space-time continuum creaking under the strain.

"You're all here, too? You came over, huh?"

"What's going on, Hanuki?" asked Jogasaki in bewilderment. "What's got you so jazzed?"

"Hold up, Jogasaki. How can you be so composed? Unbelievable. Are you savoring this moment? Are you savoring this invaluable experience?"

"Savoring what?"

"What a pain in the butt you are. You're allowed to have emotions, you know!"

I realized Hanuki was in the grip of a fatal misunderstanding.

When she had boarded the time machine, Jogasaki, Aijima, Akashi, and I were present. And now, the exact same lineup was here. She was under the impression we had all come from tomorrow.

I fairly leaped over to her. "You're drunk, huh, Hanuki?"

"How rude. I can't be drunk."

"That's what all drunk people say."

Akashi ran over, too, and signaled Hanuki with her eyes. "Hanuki, let's go sober up."

"But I'm not drunk . . ."

"You are. You're absolutely wasted. Let's go."

We dragged Hanuki away from there. From behind us we could hear Jogasaki muttering, totally lost, "I have no idea what's going on."

At any rate, thanks to Hanuki's extraordinarily bold interruption, we were lucky enough to dodge Jogasaki's suspicions. When we got to the stairs, Hanuki shook her arm free and whined, "What the hell? Ugh."

"That's my line," I said. "The universe nearly disappeared."

"What? What are you talking about?"

"That was Jogasaki and Aijima from yesterday," Akashi said, and Hanuki's eyes went huge.

"What? Really? They didn't come on the time machine?"

"Only Akashi and I came after you all. Plus, you can tell by looking. Jogasaki was dressed like Saigo Takamori."

"Ohhh, right. Sorry, sorry."

"Please be more careful!" When I gave her a stern warning, Hanuki made a pouty face.

"You don't have to bite my head off."

"Except one small screwup could destroy the universe."

"Yes, that—what's that all about?"

We didn't have time to go through the whole explanation. When I asked where Ozu and Higuchi were, she said, "They said they're going to stake out Oasis," with a laugh. "Higuchi wants to figure out who stole his shampoo. It's so idiotic."

I had sort of seen it coming, but even so, the astonishing lack of concern this idiot master-disciple pair displayed made my head spin.

"Do they *want* to destroy the universe?"

"Let's go get them," said Akashi, taking the lead and heading down the stairs. But as we reached the landing, she stopped short and said, "We can't go this way."

There were a ton of chatty voices coming from the first-floor entryway. Apparently, the film crew had returned. With no other choice, we ran back up and hid in the communal bathroom next to the stairs. As we waited behind the door with bated breath, a crowd of people stomped up to the second floor.

We could hear Akashi and me from yesterday talking to each other.

"Are you guys going to Oasis?"

"Yeah, what about you, Akashi?"

"Once things are cleaned up, I'm going to go to the used book fair."

Right, I remembered having that conversation after we finished filming. It was like déjà vu, except not. A true repetition.

"Is that what my voice sounds like? I sound so weird."

"I don't think you sound weird."

"No, I definitely sound weird." Akashi got extremely self-conscious.

Suddenly, someone tried to come into the bathroom. I immediately clenched the doorknob, threw my weight against the door, and held my ground. After a moment, we heard Ozu say, "Um, I can't get into the bathroom." Leisurely footsteps flip-flopped closer.

"Did you break the door?" Higuchi asked.

"Don't be ridiculous!" Ozu answered.

They combined their strengths to try to force the door open, so all three of us pushed back.

Eventually they seemed to give up.

"Well, whatever. I'll go at the bathhouse."

"You're planning on wearing that makeup to the bathhouse?"

"It's creepy, right? Masterfully creepy, if I say so myself. Don't you think it would be creepy if I wore this while twitching in the electric bath?"

"I can think of nothing creepier."

"Then let's get going, Master."

"No, hold your horses. I need to get my Vidal Sassoon."

Following that surprisingly substanceless conversation, Higuchi and Ozu moved away from the bathroom.

I opened the door a crack and checked to make sure there was no one nearby before saying, "Come on."

Just before going down the stairs, I looked down the hallway, which was as crowded as a station platform, and spotted myself leaning against the wall. I (from yesterday) was standing right in front of me; it was an eerie, novel experience. What would happen if I called out to me (from yesterday)? As I was staring in fascination, I (from yesterday) turned to look our way. I managed to hide just in time.

Akashi turned to me from the landing and hissed, "Hurry!"
I rushed down the stairs.

• • •

We exited the apartment building into the scorching residential neighborhood just before four p.m. The sun cast dark shadows at our feet, and cicadas were crying in the trees lining the street.

It's just like déjà vu, I thought.

But it wasn't déjà vu; it was unmistakably a repetition.

"So that's what that was about." Akashi nodded to herself as she walked briskly along in the dappled light beneath the trees. "Yesterday after we broke down the set, Jogasaki and Aijima were acting strange. They looked at me weird and seemed sort of scared of me. But now the mystery's solved. They had met the me from the future."

"So the flow of time is aligned?"

"I think so."

But something was bothering me.

What was bothering me was Hanuki's unprecedented adventure.

According to what she told me on the way to the bathhouse, when she, Ozu, and Higuchi had arrived in the time machine about an hour ago, she decided to split from the other two and infiltrate the *Lives of Bakumatsu Weaklings* filming.

"This is what makes time machines so useful!"

Flitting across the back of my mind was the Hanuki who had showed up at the end of filming to swagger around. She gave notes on Higuchi's acting from behind the camera, helped touch up Ozu's face paint, passed out lukewarm Calpis drinks to the crew, and so on. The shocking truth, so nonchalantly revealed, was that that had been future Hanuki!

"But the flow of time is aligned, right? Because I was actually at the filming 'yesterday.'"

True, the flow of time was aligned. But would this really be good enough?

The closest bathhouse, Oasis, was down Mikage-dori away from Shimogamo Izumikawacho and across the Takano River to the east, in a residential area. Between the curtain with just the character *yu*—for bathwater—left undyed, the elevated custodian's seat, and the big baskets lined up in the changing rooms, it was truly the Platonic ideal of a public bathhouse; and just as this paragraph was repeated, so too was the bathhouse a total repetition.

At some point, Jogasaki, Higuchi, Ozu, and I would show up. Before yesterday-us caught up to us, we had to get future Higuchi and Ozu out of there.

But as we were about to duck under the curtain, I stopped.

"Hanuki, you were at Oasis yesterday, right?"

Hanuki replied in annoyance, "You asked me that before, too, but I already told you, I didn't go to the bathhouse."

But that made no sense. I had definitely heard her voice the previous day. Hadn't she called out to Higuchi and Jogasaki from the women's bath?

Maybe that had been Hanuki from the future?

If so, we had a bit of a problem. Taking Higuchi and Ozu back wouldn't be enough. Hanuki would have to go into the women's bath and call out to us (from yesterday) in the men's area later. The only answer to the question of why she had to do that was "because that's how it was yesterday."

As usual, Hanuki made a sour face at my suggestion. "No, I'm not doing that. Too much work."

"But you were in the women's bath yesterday . . ."

"Except I wasn't! Don't make me say it again!"

It was precisely because she wasn't there yesterday that she had to go in today. Otherwise the flow of time wouldn't align.

I pleaded with her about how dangerous it was to alter the past with the time machine. One false move and not only Hanuki and I but the entire universe would disappear. The fate of the cosmos hung on whether Hanuki went into the bath or not at this moment. Thanks to Akashi jumping in to assist me, Hanuki finally assented, though still suspicious. "If I have to . . ."

I explained the interaction we'd had at Oasis yesterday. I was worried about whether Hanuki would say the right thing, but then Akashi said, "I memorized it. I'll go with her, so there's no need to worry."

"I'm counting on you, Akashi."

"Leave it to me." She nodded.

With that, we ducked under the entrance curtain at Oasis.

$$\bullet\ \bullet\ \bullet$$

The usual elderly custodian was napping on the job.

This guy was almost always asleep, so this place was no different from an unstaffed bathhouse.

Leaving the fee next to him, I looked around the changing room. How many times had I seen this area since moving into Shimogamo Yusuiso? Clothing baskets lined up on wooden shelves, a fridge filled with coffee-flavored milk and green juice, a noisy fan, an untrustworthy piece-of-junk scale.

I called out to the ominous darkness in the corner of the changing room.

"Hey, Ozu. What are you doing here?"

The yokai Nurarihyon had flopped into a massage chair and was emitting a *nngh-gh-gh-gh* with his eyes rolled back. This massage chair, a deleterious masterpiece that after use immediately rendered one unwell, was known far and wide as one of the Three Great Torture Devices that Oasis boasted, along with the Killer Electric Bath and Dr. Agriculture's Funky Green Juice. Even in all of Sakyo Ward, the only person who could possibly want to inflict such suffering on himself was that embodiment of the dark actuality of humanity, Ozu.

Ozu noticed me and sat up cheerfully. "Oh, you're here, too? Welcome to yesterday. How did you like your ride on the time machine?"

"Never mind that. Where's the AC remote?"

"You needn't worry. I've got it right here." He pulled the remote out of a pocket in his pants and reverently offered it to me.

When I took it, I was simultaneously hit with relief and a deep sadness. This remote was a magic wand that would unlock the door to our glorious future. Yet I had to say a requiem for it instead. What can you call that besides a tragedy?

"I'm putting this back where you found it."

"Why? After all the trouble we went through to get it!"

"Using the time machine irresponsibly could cause the universe to disappear. You guys should stop whatever pointless thing you're doing and come straight back to tomorrow. Where's Higuchi?"

"He's already on the stakeout. In the bath."

I crossed the changing room and opened the glass door. In the afternoon sun shining in through the skylight, Higuchi was soaking in the large bath on the right-hand side. He leisurely raised a hand and said, "You came, too, my good sir?" His perfectly chill demeanor had none of the tension of a stakeout. I asked him to get out immediately, but he just shook his head and said, "No can do."

"I'll carry you out of here if I have to. Ozu, gimme a hand." When I turned around I nearly shrieked. "What the—? Why'd you take your clothes off?"

"To get into the bath, of course."

"Did you not understand a word I said?"

"We're about to catch the thief who stole Master's shampoo. Gotta make good use of the time machine."

Ozu shoved me aside and got into the bath.

All I could think was that both Higuchi and Ozu were both agents of evil plotting to destroy the universe. The clock in the changing room read 4:15 p.m. It would be less than five minutes before yesterday-us showed up for our bath.

Standing at the entrance to the bathing area in a daze, I suddenly realized something weird. When we had come the previous day, there had been three other customers. They all had towels wrapped tightly around their heads and were sitting with their backs to the tub, endlessly washing up. I remembered them well because they were so strange. But now, nobody was around except Higuchi, Ozu, and me. *When are those three guys going to show up? There's hardly any time left . . .*

Having thought that far, it finally hit me. Grabbing three towels, I took my clothes off, jumped into the bath, and dragged Higuchi and Ozu out.

"Wrap these towels around your heads! Hurry up!"

When we sat in a row facing the showers, *we* were those three strange bathers—the shady guys I had seen in the bath the previous day.

"Don't let yesterday-us notice us," I said. "If they do, the universe goes poof."

"But we need to catch the shampoo thief."

"That's right. Scoundrels need to be pounded with the iron hammer of justice."

"Higuchi, I'll buy you some new shampoo, so just—"

"That's not the issue here. This is a question of what's right."

There were voices coming from behind the glass door. Talk about the nick of time. When I looked over, I saw Jogasaki (from yesterday) paying the fee. The rest of us (from yesterday) followed.

"They're here," I said.

• • •

We (from yesterday) spaced out soaking in the large tub.

"*Chu chu tako kai na.*" Ozu sang a strange song.

"*Lives of Bakumatsu Weaklings* seems like it'll be a pretty interesting movie, huh?"

"I think not." Jogasaki groaned.

"Oh? You're not happy with it, Jogasaki?"

"How could I be? I'll never approve of such a trashy movie."

"Akashi was pretty satisfied."

"A film is an appeal to society and should be made with more sincerity. The script alone was a shit show. You're making a mockery of the people around you by even thinking about making a movie out of that. I think she's wasting her talent."

"I mean, it's an amateur film either way."

"Guys like you are going to send our culture into decline."

"At any rate, my performance was undeniably brilliant." Higuchi suddenly tooted his own horn. "It's the dawn of Japan!"

That was the conversation unfolding as I scrubbed myself in silence near the wall, ears sharp. *What a bunch of carefree dopes*, I even thought in anger. *Cultural decline? The dawn of Japan? If the universe disappears, none of that will even matter.*

Higuchi was scrubbing noisily to my left as he peeked at the scene behind us. Despite the impending cosmic crisis, all he could think about was the shampoo thief.

"The Vidal Sassoon seems to still be in my bucket."

"Higuchi, please just leave it."

"What's the point of a time machine if we don't seize this opportunity?"

In this men's bath, there were two of me, Ozu, and Higuchi. And we were all naked. If we couldn't manage to keep the existence of this trio of unsightly pairs a secret, our universe would have no future. And in the women's bath next door, Hanuki and Akashi were standing by to make sure the flow of time aligned. The old custodian surely never imagined that the continued existence of the cosmos hinged on events unfolding in his bathhouse.

Horrifyingly, Higuchi (from yesterday) eventually emerged from the bath and sat down to the left of Higuchi (from today) and started washing himself.

Not only that, but they started to exchange trivial small talk.

"It's nice to go to the bathhouse in the summer, 'ey?"

"I couldn't agree more."

"Of course, it's nice to go to the bathhouse in the winter, too."

"Yes, I couldn't agree more about that, either. Great minds."

Seized by a fear that the universe was warping, I furiously poked Higuchi (from today) in the flank, but he didn't seem to care. Higuchi and Higuchi were getting along famously; they even shook hands.

Higuchi (from yesterday) held out his Vidal Sassoon. "This is some great shampoo. Try it out."

"Oh, thanks, I appreciate it."

Higuchi (from today) took the shampoo and gazed at it lovingly. Higuchi (from yesterday) was looking down as he petted his leg hair. I was going out of my mind.

Just then we heard an amorous voice coming from the women's bath.

"Higuchiii! Jogasakiii!"

"Oh?" Higuchi (from yesterday) looked up at the ceiling. "Is that Hanuki? I never see you here!"

"I thought I'd like to go take a bath for a change." Hanuki's easygoing voice echoed.

"Good idea. Such things give life some elegance."

The relief I felt hearing Hanuki's brilliant performance lasted but a moment. When Higuchi (from yesterday) began washing his hair, Higuchi (from today) flung off his head towel and began washing his, too. Once the shower washed the suds away, it would be clear at a glance that they were the same person.

That was when I (from yesterday) stood up and went to leave the bathtub.

"I'm going to go back ahead of you guys. I have an errand to run," I heard him say.

"Leaving so soon?" said Ozu (from yesterday), twitching in the electric bath. "You should relax, take your time."

The Ozu on my right spoke into my ear. "I was wondering about that yesterday. Why'd you leave so suddenly?"

"It was nothing. I just had an errand to run."

"Oh-ho?"

"I'm a bit busy at the moment. Could you shut up?"

"It was a woman, wasn't it?"

I stared at him in shock.

"Bingo," he murmured as he slithered creepily up and out of his seat. "I see. If that's how it is, then I'm going to tail yesterday-you."

"No!" I tried to grab him, but he slipped away and headed

for the changing room. I very much wanted to go after him, but Higuchi's identity was on the verge of being revealed. Not to mention that I (from yesterday) was in the changing room getting dressed.

While I was rinsing Higuchi's head and wrapping it back in the towel, I saw me (from yesterday) leaving the bathhouse in a hurry. I grabbed Higuchi's arm and went across the bathing area. But I was a hair late, and just as we were heading into the changing room, Ozu went flying out of the bathhouse. I'll never forget the demonic grin he flashed when he turned back just before ducking under the curtain.

As I was stomping my feet in a rage, Higuchi said, "Don't be irritated, my good sir."

"And who's the one irritating me?"

"Oh, don't be angry. I'll go quietly." He smugly held up the bottle of Vidal Sassoon. "I decided to steal it before it got stolen. So the flow of time will align, right?"

True, the flow of time was aligned. But would this really be good enough?

Higuchi's Vidal Sassoon was stolen at the bathhouse yesterday. That was why he came here in the time machine. But the perpetrator of the crime was that very Higuchi who came in the time machine. Higuchi stole from Higuchi, and the Higuchi who was stolen from stole from Higuchi. How was I supposed to deal with this paranoid conflict transcending time and space?

As I was standing there dumbfounded, Higuchi began to leisurely dress himself.

It was all mind-bogglingly idiotic, but I looked up at the

ceiling of the changing room and took a deep breath. "This is fine," I murmured. *As Higuchi said: the flow of time will align. I have no reason to complain. Even if the whole thing is a waste of time, as long as the flow of time aligns, it's fine. I'm not going to worry about this anymore.*

I hurriedly dressed and headed for the custodian's seat. Before a towering stack of change, the old man was still contentedly napping.

"Akashi, are you there?"

She peeked around the partition. "Did everything go okay?"

"Yes."

"Who was the shampoo thief?"

"I'll tell you later. More importantly," I said, handing her the AC remote. "Ozu had it, as I thought. Put it back where it was, will you?"

"You're not going back?"

"I need to go catch Ozu. You head back to the apartment and return Higuchi and Hanuki to the future. They're way too risky."

Akashi nodded before giving me a concerned look. "But where did Ozu go?"

"I know where he is."

• • •

When I left the bathhouse, the long twilight of August was just beginning.

"Crap, crap, crap," I grumbled as I headed west on Mikage-dori.

Let's recall what happened yesterday: As I was on my way back to Shimogamo Yusuiso after leaving the bathhouse, I caught sight of Akashi heading to the used book fair. "This is a once-in-a-lifetime chance!" I said, and went after her in high spirits, meaning to invite her to watch the Gozan Okuribi with me, but I ended up choosing an honorable retreat.

"I'm going to tail yesterday-you." That's what Ozu had said when he left Oasis.

August 11, four thirty p.m.: I was following Ozu, who was following me, who was following Akashi.

I had to catch up to Ozu no matter what. If I didn't, he would witness me in all my valiance beating a dejected retreat from the used book fair after failing to ask Akashi out. That would already be mortifying enough to defy expression, but the real problem would be Ozu's behavior after witnessing that human comedy. There was no way a man who boasted that he fueled himself on other people's misfortunes would quietly watch over me from the shadows. He would definitely forget himself in his amusement and commit some kind of outrage that would obliterate the order of space-time.

Destruction over creation—that was Ozu's creed.

• • •

I first met Ozu in the Keifuku Electric Railroad Research Society at school.

You would think from the name that we were a bunch of train otaku, but our interests were different from so-called railroad enthusiasts. That is, the group had been formed on the hypothesis that there was once a Keifuku line connecting Kyoto and Fukui; it was an imaginary train club. According to club lore, the Randen, Eiden, and the Fukui Keifuku lines were once connected in one big, long line called the Saba Kaido. You can find remains of the Saba Kaido scattered around town.

This is 100 percent tall tale, so you mustn't believe a word of it, wise readers.

The main activities of the Keifuku Electric Railroad Research Society were following "traces of the abandoned tracks" and discovering "relics" from the time they existed. The members of the club were all men of great perception; they would find remains everywhere they went, whether in the city or in the woods. After a few hours of devoted surveying, we would meet at our usual izakaya to review. It was our custom that whoever made the most plausible find of the day would be treated to a beer. I had that honor the day I made the amazing discovery of the train shed for the "saba cars" that transported seafood from Fukui to Kyoto. In short, the Keifuku Electric Railroad Research Society was a supremely intellectual diversion for mature individuals wherein we fantasized about an imaginary train line based on a daydream hypothesis.

It was mid-May, and the club had just added two eccentric new students. After finishing our survey among the fresh greenery on Mount Kurama, we went to an izakaya near Demachiyanagi Station to have a welcome party. Following the ceremonial presentation of a beer to the person who had made the most plausible find, and after the new students had introduced themselves, it was Ozu who said, "Hey everyone, what if we did something daring this year? Let's compile our research into a zine and sell it at the school festival."

The idea was to share the romance of the Saba Kaido far and wide.

At first, there were those who urged caution. The Saba Kaido was a train line of the heart that existed inside each of us individually. All these Saba Kaido were different, and they were all good. But if we were to compile a zine, we would have to force them to converge into an objective form, and the discrepancies between our individual fantasies would come into sharp relief. That would damage the society's spirit of freedom.

In retrospect, this take was exactly right.

That spring and summer, the atmosphere of the Keifuku Electric Railroad Research Society steadily worsened.

Obviously, the cause was Ozu's suggestion of creating a zine. The idea of a zine triggered conflict between the images of a "realistic," "rational," "profitable" Saba Kaido that had begun coalescing in the members' minds. They had all been perfect gentlemen and respected one another's fantasies up to this point, but now they began finding fault with the others' conceptions: "That's not realistic." "That's not rational." "That wouldn't turn a profit."

Around the time of Gion Matsuri, Ozu visited me at Shimogamo Yusuiso, and I told him, "I smell trouble."

"Seriously, though. What's gotten into everyone?"

"I'm pretty sure it's your fault. Take responsibility."

"All I did was propose what I thought was a good idea,"

he said, sounding carefree. "Well, these things happen sometimes. We're only human."

But as we headed into summer vacation, not only did the antagonism between members show no signs of abating, but the zine wasn't coming together, either. And everyone ignored me when I said we should scrap it. The other guys must have thought, *I'm not about to back down now!* I went around trying to bridge the gap and advocate harmony, but I only ended up getting criticized: "You don't even have a horse in this race, so you can't talk."

And the one at the vanguard of the reproach was none other than the guy who had urged caution, lamenting that we could lose our free spirit. Somewhere along the way he had turned into a fault-finding machine, constantly attacking everyone around him with combative language. In early autumn, his bad-mouthing had gotten so nasty that he was practically run out of the club, leading him to establish the Keifuku Electric Railroad Society Fukui Faction, but the infighting didn't fizzle out there. The remaining members split into the Randen Faction and the Eiden Factions, and they argued bitterly; the subject of the school festival didn't even come up anymore.

Eventually the Randen Research Society and the Eiden Research Society went independent, and the only two of the original club left were me and Ozu. That said, by that point I was over all the internal strife, so I had cut ties with everyone and was holed up in my room in Shimogamo Yusuiso.

At the end of November, at about the time the cold started to really bite, I was frying up a fish burger on an electric burner all by my lonesome when Ozu dropped by. We stayed up late drinking.

"There's no one left."

"There's nothing for me and you to do together. Let's disband."

"Ugh, I suppose we might as well."

Thus, the club once known as the Keifuku Electric Railroad Research Society ceased to exist.

However, this chronicle of its rise and fall has an epilogue.

In mid-December, the Keifuku Electric Railroad Research Society Fukui Faction, which had been lying low surveying in Fukui, reached out to the Randen Research Society and the Eiden Research Society for reconciliation. The school festival had long since ended, so apparently it felt ridiculous to continue arguing about the content of the zine.

Responding to this invitation, the former members of the Keifuku Electric Railroad Research Society met at an izakaya at the Hyakumanben intersection, and it was as if whatever had been possessing them had been exorcized. At their first dinner in a while, having the opportunity to speak honestly with one another, they realized that Ozu had been secretly fanning the flames of their discord.

When they took a close look at the progression of their strife, it was Ozu who had chased off the radicalized Fukui Faction, and it was Ozu who had set the Randen and Eiden Factions against each other. And wasn't the whole root of the thing his zine proposal?

"Was it all just a scheme?"

"That dude's like the devil."

"But Ozu's gone. There's no reason to argue anymore."

So it was that the Keifuku Electric Railroad Research Society Fukui Faction absorbed the Randen and Eiden Research Societies to become the new Keifuku Electric Railroad Research Society. Having overcome an era of miserable infighting, their friendship had only grown stronger. The members all swore they would never again be taken in by a villain like Ozu.

And they all lived happily ever after.

Ozu told me about it early in the new year when I ran into him at the co-op bookstore.

". . . so I guess that's where things stand now."

"Hey, what the hell?" I had been left out completely.

Though it might have been a bit of a rough trial, I think we can say that the internal strife was a meaningful experience for the Keifuku Electric Railroad Research Society. "After rain comes fair weather," as they say. Surely the memory of the absurd conflict that drove the club to collapse would be recounted in perpetuity; it would be a cautionary tale for anyone defending the spirit of freedom. All's well that ends well . . . is what I'd like to say, but do you really think that's how it played out? What about me? Not that I felt like rejoining the Keifuku Electric Railroad Research Society at that point.

That winter, I holed up in my four-and-a-half-mat tatami room, cradling an electric heater like a brazier and raging, *After all my calls for harmony!* They hadn't listened to me one bit, only said, "You don't even have a horse in this race, so you can't talk"; so it rubbed me the wrong way that when the era of chaos ended, they could just blame everything on Ozu and be like, "Let's all be friends!"

If they come apologize to me, I guess I can forgive them! I thought.

But not a single person came.

Only Ozu was left.

• • •

"We're connected by the black thread of fate" is what Ozu says.

It had already been two and a half years since I started university, and after wandering my four-and-a-half-mat tatami wasteland, all I got was a fatal bond with this weirdo.

What could it possibly mean? Did I make a mistake somewhere along the way? Was I at fault? I at least wanted to be with someone whose spirit was a bit more kindred (or a black-haired maiden).

I finally caught up with Ozu after crossing Mikagebashi. Along Mikage-dori heading toward Tadasu no Mori, a chase like a loop of prayer beads was in progress. At the rear was Ozu hiding behind a utility pole; walking ahead of him was me (from yesterday) with my bath bucket; and walking ahead of *him* was Akashi (from yesterday). Before long, Akashi (from yesterday) turned right down the approach to Shimogamo Shrine. I (from yesterday) went right after her.

As Ozu watched everything from behind the utility pole, his shoulders shook in amusement. "Ooh-hoo-hoo."

When I snuck behind him and grabbed his arm, he whirled around in shock.

"What! You already caught up to me?"

"All right, we're leaving."

"Hang on—just a little longer." He squirmed. "Things are about to get interesting."

"There's nothing the least bit interesting about this. Get your ass back to the future—now."

"Nah, nah, you can't pull the wool over my eyes. That's Akashi walking over there. And that's you behind her. What the heck are you up to?"

Seeing my inability to produce an answer, Ozu's face lit up.

"I gotta see this!"

He wriggled out of my grasp. My hand shot out but caught only air, which caused me to lose balance and fall on my butt. Ozu took that opportunity to race down Mikage-dori.

"Get back here!" I shouted, but he paid me no mind and disappeared into Tadasu no Mori.

Night had crept into the forest early. When I entered from the side, off the long approach to Shimogamo Shrine, a great many white tents were lining both sides of the riding grounds that stretched north to south. Shoppers had grown sparse, and a loudspeaker was announcing closing time. But Ozu was nowhere to be found. I walked speedily from tent to used bookstore tent.

It was no trouble to find Akashi (from yesterday) and me (from yesterday).

Akashi was flitting between bookshelves at furious whirl-wind pace, and I pursued with a grimace of desperation. I was just like a small-time villain in a Western getting dragged around after being lassoed by a cowgirl on her horse.

Yesterday I had been under the impression that I was following her "nonchalantly."

But now, watching objectively, I could see that I looked totally shady. I kept glancing around with zero composure; no sooner had I picked up a book than I would put it back and dash off, only to stop again and hide behind a shelf. Shoppers passing by looked at me with suspicion, and the bookstore staff clearly thought I was shoplifting. But even those frowning shopkeepers, when they realized I was following Akashi, smiled weakly with a knowing "Oh-ho" or "Aha."

Watching over me (from yesterday) from behind a bookcase, I was practically pulling my hair out in agony. *Please quit parading this disgrace around for all to see.* If it were possible, I would have wanted to run over to me (from yesterday), tap him on the shoulder, and tell him, "Just give up already!"

Eventually, yesterday-me's footsteps slowed down. More and more space opened up between him and Akashi, and finally, he stopped in his tracks. In the center of the riding grounds, surrounded on either side by tents, he stood in a daze with a self-deprecating grin on his face.

As I was standing behind a bookcase thinking, *Oh brother*, someone suddenly clapped my shoulder from behind.

"I see. So that's what happened," Ozu sidled up to me in satisfaction and whispered into my ear. I didn't even feel like making excuses anymore.

"This shame will live on for generations," I groaned.

"Haven't you always been the type of guy whose shame

would live on for generations? What good would it do to start fixing things now? This is training to become a bigger person," Ozu said, casting his gaze to me (from yesterday) standing in the center of the riding grounds. "What is he thinking about so hard right now?"

I could remember quite vividly what I (from yesterday) was thinking:

(i) It was impossible to naturally strike up a conversation with Akashi.
(ii) I would feel bad bothering her.
(iii) I hadn't managed to get any closer to her at all.

It's very strange, but the moment I saw me (from yesterday) give up on pursuing her, an intense anger surged within me: *Why are you backing down now?!*

If it were possible, I would have wanted to run over to yesterday-me, tap him on the shoulder, and tell him, *Just keep following her.* I (from yesterday) didn't know that this strategic retreat was an irreparable failure. He was thinking, *I'll call it a day.* He was thinking, *There's always tomorrow.* But that tomorrow would never come.

"Huh?" Ozu murmured in concern. "Looks like you're turning back."

I (from yesterday) turned on my heel and trudged south.

As I was watching that pathetic me go, Ozu slipped out of a used bookstore tent.

He went to the center of the riding grounds and gazed south toward me (from yesterday) in disgust. Then he turned north to watch Akashi speed away. North, south, north again. His gaze flipped back and forth like a rattle drum. When he was about to hurry south, I barred his path.

"Wait, hold up. What are you trying to do?"

"You weren't thinking 'I'll call it a day,' were you?"

"This is the end," I fairly spat, and his eyes went large.

"Hold on a second. You invited her to the Gozan Okuribi, didn't you?"

"No, I didn't."

"Then who invited her?"

"How should I know?"

Ozu looked up at the golden sky and heaved a sigh. "I'm sure you were making excuses like 'This is a strategic retreat' and 'There's always tomorrow.' And as a result, some random nobody beat you to it . . . You should be absolutely ashamed of yourself!"

"Hey, stop telling me what I need to hear."

"You should be at least a little frustrated about this."

"Doesn't matter if I am or not at this point. There's no way to fix it."

"No, c'mon. There's absolutely a way to fix it."

Ozu twisted his lips into a smile. It was the exact expression of a villainous merchant in a period film handing a bribe over to the acting administrator—not the type of face that should be allowed in a sacred forest.

"Today you should just invite her on behalf of yesterday-you," he said. "What else is a time machine for?"

"You lack a fundamental understanding of the issue. That sort of thing isn't allowed!"

True, we were in possession of a time machine. But if the slightest alteration to the past could cause the universe to collapse, then what could we do? If my strategic retreat from the used book fair was in the past, then someone inviting Akashi was also in the past. Just like the Coke-soaked remote, they were both irreversible at this point.

In reality, a time machine isn't good for anything. It's too dangerous; you can't use it even if you want to.

But even when I argued along those lines, Ozu just made a face like a horse reacting to a Buddhist prayer.

"So you're giving up?"

"What choice do I have?"

"Fine. I get it." He shoved me aside and walked south.

"Hey, where are you going?"

"If today-you is giving up, then I'll go convince yesterday-you."

"I'm *telling* you, if you do that, the universe will be destroyed!"

"We don't know if it'll be destroyed or not unless we give it a shot!"

He dashed off with those horrific parting words.

I ran after Ozu. Plowing through alarmed passersby who asked what was going on, I leaped and tackled him from behind.

"Fight! Fight!" people began to shout.

A sudden tension shot through the book fair, and men rushed over from various directions.

Voices called out, "Hey, hey, calm down" and "What's the matter?" but no one jumped in to stop us. Our struggle was so impotent, they couldn't even be sure it really was a fight, so apparently it was just an awkward moment: not worth getting physically involved, but impossible to just watch in silence.

Clinging to Ozu's waist, I screamed, "I wish I could have a do-over, too!"

But I was the one responsible for the failure at the used book fair yesterday. The one who feared a definitive answer and retreated with the excuse "There's always tomorrow" was me. Exposing the universe to the risk of obliteration in order to smooth over a personal error would be entirely too arrogant. No matter how precious Akashi was, destroying the universe over her was a nonstarter. *In order to protect this universe she lives in, I have to accept the consequences of my foolish actions. That's youth; that's life.*

Thinking those things made me want to cry.

I shoved Ozu away and prostrated myself on the damp ground. "Please, I'm begging you! Can you just come back with me without making a fuss?"

Ozu dropped to his knees and fell silent in shock.

Everyone surrounding us seemed to be holding their breath. Eventually a bookseller wearing a name tag that said Gabi Shobo walked over. He was a bald guy with an octopus-red face.

"Hey, you. I don't know what's going on, but . . ." the Gabi Shobo shopkeeper said gently to Ozu. "He's gone this far. Why don't you let it go?"

• • •

Dragging Ozu along, I left Tadasu no Mori.

"It was just a joke. I didn't think you would take it seriously!"

"You're a pain in the ass! You literally are a pain in my ass!"

"Why bring that up now? We both know already."

After rolling around on the ground, we were both filthy.

Still, our immediate problem was solved. Akashi had gone back to the apartment ahead of me, so she should have already sent Higuchi and Hanuki back. All that was left was for Ozu and me to return to tomorrow. I swore that once we got back, I would pack Tamura off to the future as quickly as possible and never go near a time machine ever again.

Shimogamo Yusuiso was so quiet it might as well have been abandoned.

It was just after five p.m. It seemed as though all the members of the Ablutions film club had gone home.

We cautiously slipped into the building through the front door. The dusty hallway leading away from the entrance was so dark it was like one of those haunted tunnels. When we went up the stairs, the faint light streaming in from the laundry-drying area made it possible to see a slim figure sitting alone on the couch.

When I said, "We're back," Akashi sprang to her feet.

I could tell something was off at a glance. She was much paler than usual, and her hands were clasped tightly at her chest. I had a bad feeling. She must have run into some trouble.

"The time machine hasn't come back!" she said, jogging over to us. "When I sent the master and Hanuki back, I made them promise to return the time machine right away. But it's been fifteen minutes already, and nothing. And not only that—"

"It's okay, Akashi. Calm down—"

"But—"

"It's all right. The flow of time is aligned. There's no more cosmic crisis. Even if the time machine doesn't come back, we can just return on our own."

"No! None of that is true!" She shook her head in irritation. "The remote is gone!"

"What? How?" I had the feeling the ground we'd firmly planted our feet on had begun to crumble. "I thought I took it back from Ozu and gave it to you!"

"The master took it back to the future!"

While Ozu and I were scuffling at the used book fair in Tadasu no Mori, Akashi had been taking Hanuki and Higuchi back to Shimogamo Yusuiso.

Her highest priority was to put the A/C remote I'd entrusted to her back on top of the fridge in the hallway. That was where the remote would meet its end bathed in Coke. Then they went to the laundry-drying area and carried in the time machine.

"Once you get there, please send the machine back."

When Akashi pressed her point, Hanuki agreed. "Got it."

And just as the time machine was taking off, Higuchi reached his hand out.

"Oh, I almost forgot. Akashi, can you grab the remote for me?"

He said it as if it were the most natural request in the world. Akashi was barely conscious of herself grabbing the remote off the fridge and handing it to him. "Here you go."

She realized she'd made a terrible mistake just as the time machine disappeared without a trace.

When she finished telling us this development, she looked so dejected I felt sorry for her.

"I'm sorry. That screwup will haunt me for the rest of my life."

"Higuchi just didn't get it on a fundamental level, huh."

"A fatal error at a critical juncture! Guess the universe is gonna collapse and it's all Akashi's fault."

When Ozu rubbed salt into her wound, she hung her head like a broken marionette. Then she turned to the wall and murmured, "I don't know how I can ever apologize enough," as she began clonking her head against it. "I'm so sorry, inhabitants of the universe."

"It wasn't only you, though. All of us who used the time machine are to blame," I told Akashi. "And we still have time."

That said, the time we had wasn't much. Eventually Akashi (from yesterday) would return from the used book fair and Higuchi and the guys (from yesterday) would get back from Oasis. Plus Hanuki (from yesterday) would show up after she got off work. Once everyone else was gathered and I (from yesterday) returned from licking my wounds by the bank of the Kamo River, the fated Coke Incident would occur. If the remote wasn't here by then, the universe would be done for.

"First we have to wait for the time machine to come back."

It was a truly vexing time, so tense it was hard to breathe.

Akashi remained seated on the couch with her hands tightly clasped, not moving a muscle. As the light from the laundry-drying area grew weaker, her face, looking down, seemed to sink underwater the way the shadows increased. She seemed to be overwhelmed by responsibility to the universe.

You didn't do a single thing wrong, I told her in my head. It was my fault for saying we should use the time machine to come get the remote. It was Ozu's fault for spilling Coke on the remote in the first place. That's right. All responsibility lay with him.

The dusky light from the laundry-drying area made the end of the universe seem nigh. The universe was going to end over a stupid air conditioner remote. The only consolation was that Akashi was with me, but ruining that consolation was the fact that Ozu was also present.

It didn't seem to bother him that the universe was ending. "It'll all work out somehow," he said, cheerfully. His groundless optimism irritated me.

"By the way, Akashi, there's something I wanted to ask you." He suddenly turned to her. "Who are you going to the Gozan Okuribi with? Of course, I want to respect your privacy and all, but please tell me this one thing honestly."

"Hey, cut it out," I said. "We don't need to discuss that *now.*"

"What do you mean? It's tied to the fate of the universe!"

Akashi looked at him blankly.

"You are going, right?" he prodded.

"Yes, I'm going. I'm going, but . . ." she said with a glance at me. Then she clammed up.

"And?" Ozu urged her on, but she didn't say any more. What did this mysterious silence mean?

Finally, unable to take it anymore, I asked her, too. "Akashi, please, just tell us."

She looked at me incredulously. "Why would you—?"

The moment she spoke, her face was illuminated by a bluish flash. A whirlwind raged, causing the chime in the laundry-drying area to jangle wildly.

The time machine had come back.

• • •

In the end, we didn't learn who invited Akashi to the Okuribi—the reason being, a problematic bunch arrived from the future and we didn't have bandwidth to continue the conversation. Not only were Higuchi and Hanuki on the time machine that appeared in the corridor, Jogasaki, who had been so against the idea, and the dorky future human Tamura were with them.

When Hanuki announced, "We've arrived!" the hallway burst into activity.

"Why are you all here?!" I screamed.

Higuchi said, "Relax!" and clapped my shoulder. "We gave you and Akashi a hard time. Sorry. We didn't have a proper understanding of the time machine's dangers. But you don't need to worry anymore—we completely get it now."

"That's great, but you didn't all have to show up . . ."

"Strength in numbers."

"I just thought I should help if there's anything I can do . . ." said Tamura. "I feel partially responsible, as someone from the future."

"If you feel responsible, then don't do anything that isn't absolutely necessary!"

I was thinking that Jogasaki seemed awfully docile when I

noticed him sunken to the floor down the hall. Apparently he was susceptible to time machine sickness like Akashi.

Unable to feel strengthened by the numbers of this band of jolly pals, my sense of crisis only grew. They didn't have the temperance to be time travelers in the first place, and on top of that, yesterday-they would be here any minute. If this many of us all met face to face, there'd be nothing left to do but to dance till the end of the universe chanting, "E ja nai ka"—"Who cares?"

When Ozu saw Tamura, he said, "Oh, you're the guy from earlier."

"Yes, my name is Tamura. I came from the future on the time machine."

"Oh, so that's what's going on. For someone from the future, you look pretty dorky."

"Ah-ha-ha. I get that a lot. Everyone in this era is so rude."

Akashi shoved them aside and ran over to the time machine. "Where's the remote?"

"Don't worry, we made sure to bring it." Hanuki held it up triumphantly, and both Akashi and I were lost for words. It was cocooned in plastic and taped up tight. "This is what took so long. But it was a good idea, right? Now even if the soda spills, it won't break."

Akashi and I both shouted, "But we need it to break!"

"Why?"

"Because the remote broke yesterday!"

"We can't change the past!"

Hanuki made a pouty face and said, "Guess it's a no-go, Higuchi."

Higuchi stroked his stubble as he lamented. "Aww, I thought it was a good idea."

"This is why I told you not to do it." Jogasaki put a hand on the wall to stand up. "If you do that, the past will change. I told them a thousand times. These guys don't get it. It's too risky—we can't leave things up to them. I'll take charge!" With that—*eurlp*—he vomited and crumpled to the floor.

"How are you planning on taking charge?" Hanuki rubbed his back in exasperation.

In any case, we had to unwrap the remote as quickly as possible. Akashi had been fighting the good fight, but the tight, waterproof wrapping could have been the work of an artisan.

She looked up and brushed her bangs aside. "This is going to be impossible without scissors."

I flew into room 209, dug around in my desk, and returned with a pair.

At some point, Jogasaki had traded places with Akashi and gone red in the face wrestling with the remote. "Scissors," I said, but he was so focused, he didn't hear me.

"Jogasaki, please use the scissors!" said Akashi.

As we were loudly battling with the remote—"Oh-ho! The gang's all here!"—a familiar shrill voice sounded from down the hall.

Higuchi whispered, "I wonder which Aijima that is," in my ear.

"It's yesterday-Aijima," I replied with an annoyed click of my tongue. I hadn't even considered the possibility of Aijima making

an entrance. I thought he had gone straight home after the filming ended yesterday.

"Back from the bathhouse already?" Aijima asked as he approached before catching sight of the time machine. "Ohhh?"
he murmured as he examined it. "What do we have here?"

We exchanged glances in silence. Aijima gave us a dubious
look.

"This. What is this? It looks like a time machine."

"Enough about that," Akashi forcefully changed the subject, "Aijima, did you forget something?"

"No, it's just my glasses," he said without taking his eyes
off the time machine. "I change my glasses depending on
which character I'm playing. I have an easier time getting into
my roles that way. So I was wearing these glasses for filming
today, but afterward when I went to change them, I couldn't
find my usual pair."

"Aren't they in my room, then?" I whipped the door to 209
open at once. "That's where we keep the lost and found. Go
ahead, take a look."

The moment Aijima went into my room according to my
plan, I closed the door and clenched the knob.

"Why'd you close the door?" came his voice. As I held
the jiggling knob firm, I lowered my voice and said, "We got
caught! Quick, hide the time machine!"

Everyone gathered around it in confusion.

"What should we do with it?"

"Just put it out in the laundry-drying area."

"But it'll be too easy to find there."

"Why don't we send it to some other era?"

But if we only sent the time machine, it would never come back.

Higuchi said, "Leave it to me," and got into the cockpit. "I'll go off somewhere and come back a bit later."

Ozu instantly jumped abroad and said, "Allow me to accompany you!"

This seemed extremely bad, no matter how you looked at it. Giving this unprecedented duo free rein with the time machine should be properly termed blasphemy against the space-time continuum.

Jogasaki summed up my opinion. "How can we entrust the time machine to you two?!" He dragged Higuchi and Ozu off the time machine and boarded it himself.

Hanuki raced over and said, "You can't, Jogasaki! It'll make you sick again."

"If the choice is me or them, then I'm going. Don't make any extra trouble."

I'd never sympathized with Jogasaki so much. He was putting his body on the line to protect the order of time and space. Friends who stand together against adversity are bound by ties that transcend differences in status and personality.

"Come back in ten minutes," I told him, and he gave me an encouraging thumbs-up from the cockpit.

"I'll be back," he said. "You can count on me."

As the time machine began to warp, Jogasaki looked at the control panel again. Apparently, he noticed a major problem: all the blood drained from his face.

"Hey, this—!"

His pained groan cut off.

The time machine disappeared in a burst of light and wind.

• • •

When Aijima opened the door and peeked out, there was no sign of the time machine. The only trace of the whirlwind was the jangling wind chime.

"Um, the door wouldn't open," Aijima said reproachfully.

"Oh, really? That happens sometimes."

"Yeah, it seemed like someone was holding it closed."

"Why would anyone do that? Ah-ha-ha."

I signaled everyone with my eyes. Our only option was to play dumb to the last.

Higuchi, Hanuki, and Akashi were all smiles, sitting on the couch like good buddies. Ozu and Tamura were all smiles, buried in the pile of junk.

"Where'd Jogasaki go?" Aijima asked, so I said, "He remembered an urgent errand and left."

"Hey!" When Aijima came out of my room, he yelped. "The time machine's gone!"

"Time machine?"

"It was just here, wasn't it? I saw it."

"There was a time machine?"

When I cocked my head, so did everyone else.

Aijima's confidence seemed to lag. "That's so weird."

"Maybe you were dreaming."

Tamura snickered, and Aijima eyed him with suspicion.

"By the way, who are you?"

"Me?" said Tamura with a blank look.

"We've never met before, though you seem to be fitting right in . . ."

"He's Ozu's cousin." Akashi with a brilliant assist. "He's here to visit the campus over summer vacation."

"Yes, yes, that's right. My name's Tamura." Tamura got onboard with the story and put his arm around Ozu's shoulders.

When Akashi asked, "Did you find your glasses?" Aijima replied, "They're not anywhere," in annoyance and started digging through the junk in the hallway. We were anxious to get rid of him before the time machine came back. But he showed no signs of leaving and instead started chatting with Tamura.

"How did you like campus? Probably more boring than you expected, right?"

"Mmm, well, now that you mention it, I suppose."

"I mean, that's how everyone feels about it." Aijima gave a satisfied nod. "It's because you haven't explored your possibilities yet. If you decide to go here, you should make sure to go to the clock tower during the welcome season. Every kind of club imaginable will be there recruiting new members. Unlimited doors opening into the future. If you want to have a meaningful student life, join a club. You can't blaze a trail to your future as a bystander watching from the outside."

"But there's not really any club I'm interested in."

"You don't need to be interested—just join," Aijima said flatly with a glint of his glasses. "Otherwise you'll have an utterly barren four years. For instance, let's say you hole up alone in one of these four-and-a-half-mat tatami rooms. What kind of possibilities do you think you'll find? There's no romance or adventure here. There's nothing! Yesterday was the same as today, and tomorrow and today will also be the same. It's a daily life like a flavorless fish cake. Can you even call that living?"

"That's going too far," I protested firmly. "It has its own flavor."

"You only say that because you don't want to admit defeat." Aijima was merciless. "One step forward is all it takes to notice that the world is rich with possibilities—because you yourself are filled with possibilities. Your value as a human being lies precisely in that unlimited potential. Granted, I can't guarantee you'll have a rose-colored campus life. You might get tricked by a bizarre religious club or be deeply hurt after getting mixed up in your club's internal conflicts. But here's what I say: That's fine. Living out what's possible with all your might is what being young is all about!"

His grand speech was absolutely correct. As someone encircled by all manner of impossibilities, unable to leave his four-and-a-half-mat tatami room even if he wanted to, hearing those words stung.

But I couldn't just stand there being impressed; Akashi was moving in a strange way. She restlessly looked around on the floor and scanned the junk against the wall.

What's the matter? I mouthed at her.

Where is the remote? she mouthed back.

"Hey, could you look for my glasses?" Aijima said, turning

to me. "These were just for my character. I'm kinda screwed if I can't change gears. I'll come by tomorrow afternoon, so find them by then, okay?"

"Leave it to me. I'll be sure to find them." When I took on Aijima's request, he finally left.

As soon as he disappeared down the stairs, Akashi and I started a furious search.

"What's wrong?" Hanuki sat up on the couch.

"The remote's gone. It makes no sense."

Higuchi and Hanuki stood up with an "Oh crap," and Ozu and Tamura both started walking around the hallway going "Crap, crap." Then they started carelessly rummaging through the junk.

"Please be careful, everyone!" Akashi suddenly shouted. "We can't make a mess of the past!"

• • •

We completed a pass of the hallway, but all we found was Aijima's glasses; there was no sign of the AC remote. Akashi sighed.

"Jogasaki must have taken it. We were in such a hurry."

"You'd think he'd be more reliable than he is . . ." said Higuchi, and Hanuki retorted, "Nobody wants to hear that from you of all people." Then she said, "But this is really bad. We need him to come back ASAP or we'll have problems, won't we?"

It was half past five. The Coke Incident would occur in less than thirty minutes.

One thing bothering me was the strange look on Jogasaki's face just before the time machine vanished. He had seemed shocked when he looked at the control panel. As I was cocking my head wondering what that was about, Higuchi said, "The destination must have surprised him."

"Higuchi, where were you going to go?"

"Ninety-nine years ago."

No one had words.

"I thought as long as I was going to go somewhere, I might as well try the distant past," continued Higuchi. "I tried to warn him, but it was too late. It's his fault, too, though. If he was going to shove me aside, he should have at least checked where he was heading."

"Ninety-nine years ago is the Taisho era!"

"Indeed."

Just then Tamura timidly raised a hand. "Um, couldn't that be a bit of a problem? Back then, this area was a swamp. At least, that's what the landlady told me."

Back in the Taisho era, there weren't many houses in this area; it was mostly trees, rice paddies, and fields.

The current site of Shimogamo Yusuiso had been a big swamp. Weeds like long hair floated on top of the dark blue water; even during the day, the place had a ghastly vibe.

One summer evening, a man on the way back from the doctor across the river was passing by the swamp. Reflecting the sunset, it was so red it looked like a puddle of blood—even scarier than usual. As the man sped up to get past as quickly as possible, a strange voice reached his ears on the fishy breeze off the swamp water.

Eurlp, blorgh, eurrgh!

When the man looked in the direction the voice was coming from, he shivered.

In the water with the blazing glare, a freakish figure was visible. Even at a distance, it was possible to tell that the large creature was covered in dark green weeds and spitting something from its mouth as it growled, "Eurlp!" It had to be a kappa, ready to pull any passerby into the swamp.

The man practically tripped over his feet as he raced back to the village. "A kappa! There's a kappa!" he ran around shouting.

Frightening kappa rumors weren't anything new to the villagers, so they replied to the man's call immediately by arming themselves and charging toward the swamp. But just as they arrived, a blinding light flooded the area, and a tremendous wind blew all the villagers down. It was so terrifying that some of them fled.

When the strange light and wind died down, the freakish figure was gone; there was only the water gleaming red with the sunset and the fishy breeze blowing over it.

Ninety-nine years ago during the Taisho era, this apartment building didn't exist. Not only that, the ground the building was standing on didn't exist. This place had been a swamp, and the name "Yusuiso"—"Dark Water Manor," so dour for a building of apartments for students—was a reference to that history.

If Jogasaki boarded the time machine from the second floor of this building and really went to this very spot ninety-nine years ago . . .

"Maybe that kappa was Jogasaki." Tamura's comment enveloped the area in an oppressive silence.

It was then that we heard a loud noise from below.

"Maybe he's back!" said Hanuki.

We ran down the hall and peered down the stairs. It was quiet for a few moments, but then came a noise like someone slapping wet fabric against the floor. *Splat . . . splat . . . splat . . .* Coming up the stairs was a large man covered in weeds just as in the kappa legend; Jogasaki had made a safe return from the swamp of ninety-nine years ago. Carrying the time machine, he climbed the steps planting his feet one after the other.

When he reached the second floor, he slowly put the time machine on the floor.

Eurkgh! After he puked, he angrily ripped off the weeds tangled around his face. His eyes burned with rage. The next instant, he pounced violently at Seitaro Higuchi.

"Were you trying to kill me?!"

• • •

I enlisted Ozu and Tamura to help me get Jogasaki into a nelson.

"I fell into a swamp!" Swinging us three weaklings around, Jogasaki roared, "I got sick and puked! I got covered in weeds! The time machine sank! I almost died! Apologize! Apologize to me!"

The fact that he had made it back alive was a miracle, so it would be stranger for him not to be furious. Even Higuchi realized he needed to get on his hands and knees and bow. "Sorry. You're right."

"Don't you ever touch the time machine again!"

"I just wanted to try it since we had the chance."

"I'll say it one more time: Don't you ever touch the time machine again!"

Jogasaki was a pitiful sight. He was drenched in reeking swamp water and covered in muddy, dark green weeds. If you ran into him at night, you wouldn't be able to help assuming he was a yokai. It was no wonder the villagers took him for a mischievous water sprite. The origin of the kappa legend that had been told in these parts since the Taisho era was Jogasaki falling into the swamp ninety-nine years ago. But we had more pressing matters than the truth of the kappa legend.

When I said, "Jogasaki, the remote, please," he murmured, "The remote?"

"The AC remote! Then everything will be fine!"

"Ohh, that. Of course, I have it right . . ."

He put his hand in his pocket. And froze. His mouth dropped open, and his face rapidly turned white as a sheet.

"I dropped it."

"You dropped it? Where?"

"In the swamp. In that swamp."

"Ahhhhgh!" said Hanuki. "How could you, Jogasaki?"

"I was desperate just to stay alive!" he screamed miserably. "It's not my fault!"

Akashi and I slumped in a daze. The remote was now in a place we could never reach. Even if we took the time machine back ninety-nine years, how could we possibly find a remote at the bottom of a swamp? All of our efforts to protect the space-time continuum had come to nothing.

"We're done for," I murmured.

That was when Tamura thumped his fist. "Oh, I just had an idea."

"What?"

"You just need a remote for the AC, right? The AC in room 209."

"Yeah, so . . . ?"

"Got it. I'm going to use the time machine real quick."

With that he happily boarded the time machine.

"Tamura, what's your idea?"

"It's okay, I'll handle this. You can rest easy."

Tamura gave a cheery salute and left behind the familiar light and whirlwind as he vanished.

He said we could rest easy, but he was the one who had caused all this space-time trouble in the first place, so we couldn't rest, even uneasily. We exchanged extremely anxious glances. The setting sunshine streaming in from the laundry-drying area lit up Akashi's worried face. This summer "yesterday" was coming to an end.

"Akashi, about what time did you get back from the used book fair yesterday?"

"It was a little before six. The landlady's broadcast started just as I came in the entrance."

Higuchi? Seitaro Higuchi. Please come pay your rent.

She meant the Voice of the Heavens, which we would hear again the following afternoon.

Ten minutes or so after Akashi had gotten back, Higuchi, Ozu, and Jogasaki returned from the bathhouse. And while they were removing their shoes at the entrance, Hanuki showed up, having gotten off work.

"So I was the last one to get back." When I said that, everyone stared at me in confusion.

Jogasaki, Hanuki, Higuchi, Ozu, and Akashi all seemed to want to ask me what I was talking about. Something weird was going on.

"Why are you looking at me like that?" I said.

"Are you going senile?" replied Ozu. "You were the first to get back."

"Wait, what?"

"You were here when we got back from the bathhouse!"

"Maybe you're the one going senile. It's true that I was the first to leave the bathhouse, but I was running my errand after that. I didn't get home until after six, and you were all here. And then you were suddenly trying to get me to dance naked."

"Is that true?" Akashi piped up incisively. "Did you really get back after me?"

"Yeah. Why would I lie about it?" I nervously turned to her.

In the weakening light, Akashi had knit her brows and was biting her lip.

Just then, the hallway was filled with a glare and a tremendous whirlwind whipped through.

Tamura had returned.

• • •

"This thing, right?" From the cockpit, Tamura proudly presented an object.

It was the remote that was supposed to have sunk to the bottom of a swamp ninety-nine years ago.

"That's it!" Akashi pointed and screamed. "But how did you get it, Tamura?"

"I've got nothing to hide—I brought it from the future room 209."

Specifically, he went half a year past the summer he came from, to the following year's March.

When he arrived, half-a-year-later Tamura himself, along with the other members of the Shimogamo Yusuiso Time Machine Building Committee, were lined up in the hallway to meet him. They were already up to speed and had the AC remote ready for him.

"Things go pretty smoothly when you're working with your future self," Tamura laughed.

The surprising fact revealed here was that even a quarter century in the future, room 209 was still using the same air conditioner.

"But are you sure? You guys won't be able to use the AC."

"It's fine." Tamura smiled. "Actually, they're going to rebuild Shimogamo Yusuiso. The landlady has been telling us for ages to please make sure we were moved out by the end of March. And the AC unit was installed in room 209 a long time ago. It's not mine to take. Plus, it's too old. It's about time for the thing to be retired."

"So that's why you went to the end of March!"

"Yeah. There won't be anyone using it anymore."

"Tamura, you're one amazing guy."

The others chimed in with praise.

"You did a great job for a dork."

"You may be dorky, but my opinion of you has improved."

"I'm compelled to respect you despite the dorkiness."

"Everyone in this era is so rude," he winced as he got out of the time machine and solemnly handed me the remote. "Here you go. Use it however you would."

So it was that the remote came to be in my hands once more.

When I placed it on top of the fridge, there was a spontaneous round of applause.

With the remote from twenty-five years in the future filling the gap made by the remote that sank into the swamp ninety-nine years ago, the conditions of yesterday were reproduced perfectly.

For a little while, everyone kept their eyes on the remote with bated breath. The loop of cause and effect that had threatened to collapse had miraculously closed, and we had escaped the destruction of the universe. The resolution was so sudden and acrobatic.

"Won't there be trouble if we don't get out of here pretty soon?" Hanuki's question brought us back to ourselves.

Before we knew it, the twilight coming in from the laundry-drying area had nearly vanished.

Everyone rushed to board the time machine. While we were all pushing and shoving, Akashi crouched in the cockpit and spun the dial. Jogasaki elbowed Higuchi as he made his appeal: "Do *not* screw this up, Akashi!"

"Don't worry," she replied.

But even after she finished setting it up, she continued frowning at the control panel. No matter how many times we called to her, she wouldn't pull the lever. Then she abruptly stood up and said, "Something isn't right." We all lost our balance and fell in a heap.

She took my arm without a word, and as we moved away from the time machine, she lowered her voice and said, "There's something that just doesn't line up. You were here when I got back yesterday."

"But I couldn't have been. I came back last."

"So I was thinking . . . what if that you was—"

There came a grating noise from the end of the hall. The speaker in the ceiling had come on.

"Higuchi? Seitaro Higuchi. Please come pay your rent."

The landlady's solemn voice echoed.

From the time machine, the others were calling us.

"Hey, what are you guys doing?"

"Now's not the time for making out!"

"If you don't hurry up, we'll leave you here!"

Akashi waved them off in annoyance and turned back to me. "Please stay here."

"What?! Why?"

"Because this is where we made our promise yesterday!" She pleaded with her eyes. "Invite me to go see the Gozan Okuribi. Then the flow of time will align."

I heard the building's front door open downstairs. Akashi (from yesterday) had returned from the used book fair. She would come up the stairs and be here any minute. Meanwhile Akashi (from today) gave speechless me a nod, turned on her heel, ran down the hall, and leaped aboard the time machine. She waved to me.

"Do it right!"

"But, Akashi . . ."

"I'll be back for you!"

Then the time machine vanished.

I was left all alone in yesterday.

• • •

Once the flash and the whirlwind died down, the hallway was quiet.

"Because this is where we made our promise yesterday!"

It was after the time machine vanished that I finally understood what Akashi was saying.

In other words, the one who had beaten yesterday-me to making a move was today-me. I was enveloped in an inexpressibly strange sense of relief for only a split second before the terrifying weight of the responsibility I'd been given hit. If I couldn't manage to invite Akashi out properly, the flow of time wouldn't align, and the universe would be destroyed.

As I was standing there in a daze, a light went on in the darkening hallway.

"Oh, you're here?"

I turned around at the sound of the voice.

Akashi was walking down the hall toward me.

Just like an amateur actor thrust into center stage unprepared, I stared at her with my mouth only flapping in silence.

"So you're back from the bathhouse, huh? Where's Master Higuchi?" she said, but my voice wouldn't come out. She must have thought that was suspicious, because she frowned and said, "Is something wrong?"

I took a huge breath and somehow managed to say, "No, nothing."

"Really?"

"I'm okay. Just a little tired."

"Yeah, it was a full day."

"Higuchi and the guys'll be back soon. How was the book fair?"

Akashi happily lifted her bag of books to show me. "I took a quick spin around, but it wasn't enough time. I think I'll go back tomorrow."

"Right, there are a lot of shops."

"Yes. There really are so many," she said dreamily as she sat on the couch.

I leaned against the wall and looked at her. I needed to ask her out before the guys got back from Oasis. But what was the right way to go about it? It was too late to regret not asking her, herself, for details.

As I was worrying internally, she spoke. "What should my next movie be?"

"You're already thinking about the next one? That's fast."

"It's best to just forge on ahead. If I stand still, I worry," she said with a sober look on her face. "Do you have any good ideas?"

It certainly didn't feel bad to be asked. Come to think of it, the past few months I'd spent working on *Lives of Bakumatsu Weaklings* with Akashi, Ozu, and the rest of the team had been some of the brightest and most positive times in recent memory. My four-and-a-half-mat tatami room had been so gloomy since all the trouble with the Keifuku

Electric Railroad Research Society had gone down, and this project had felt like a ray of sunshine pouring in.

"How about this?" Before I knew it, I was saying, "One morning, a man wakes up in a four-and-a-half-mat tatami room. It's his usual room, but he feels uneasy for some reason. When he opens the door to go use the communal bathroom, he finds, not the hallway, but a mirror image of his room. There's a four-and-a-half-mat tatami room out the window of that room, too. No matter how far he goes, it's infinite four-and-a-half-mat tatami rooms. Without having realized it, the man had been marooned in a vast galaxy of tatami. So he sets off on a journey across the four-and-a-half-mat tatami galaxy to try to find his way back to the other world."

Akashi sat up. "Then what happens?"

"I haven't thought that far yet."

"Oh, jeez," she laughed.

"I had a dream like that once."

"You have some weird dreams," she said. "I'm jealous. All my dreams are serious."

Hold on, now's not the time to be having this conversation, I thought.

Inviting Akashi to the Gozan Okuribi would do nothing short of saving the universe. With the fate of our cosmos resting on my shoulders, taking an easy way out, like a strategic retreat, wasn't an option.

But what if I fail?

What if she says, "Why should I have to go with you?"

Why do I have to be under so much pressure? I thought. *It's just one person who finds another person desirable and* says, *"Hey, why don't we go hang out together?" Countless people have done exactly this thing thus far, and countless people will do it in the future. It's just about the most commonplace thing a person can do. Why does something so ordinary have to be so difficult?* My mouth was bone dry, and I froze up like a statue.

Akashi turned her head to listen. "Oh, seems like Master and the guys are back."

From downstairs we could hear Higuchi and Ozu's animated voices.

If that obnoxious bunch barged in here, I would lose my chance to ask Akashi out. There was no time left to hesitate. When I said "Akashi," with the mindset of jumping off a cliff, she replied with a cool, "Yes? What is it?"

"I think I'm going to go see the Gozan Okuribi this year."

"That's great."

"Would you want to come with?"

I held my breath and waited for her answer.

She was looking at me in surprise.

It was no wonder she was shocked. Why couldn't I have invited her more naturally in the flow of conversation? The few seconds of silence felt horribly long. *Is she going to turn me down? Did I fail, the way I thought I might?* I could practically see a crack forming in space before me, and I had the feeling the entire universe was going to collapse around Shimogamo Yusuiso. *Farewell, universe. Farewell, Akashi.*

The moment I had basically resigned myself to death, the cosmic crisis was averted—because Akashi nodded.

"Sure."

"Really?" I let out a huge sigh. "Okay. Good. Phew."

I was so relieved, that brusque reaction was all I could muster.

Ozu appeared from the stairwell down the hall. Higuchi, Jogasaki, and Hanuki were there, too. They seemed to be having a grand time chatting, completely unaware that I had just been waging a battle on which the fate of the universe hung. Hanuki looked our way and shouted, "Yoo-hoo!" with a wave.

"Just so I know . . ." Akashi said in a low voice as she waved back to Hanuki. "Do you mean with everyone? Or just us?"

"I'd really like to go as just us."

"I see."

"So please keep it a secret from Ozu and those guys."

"Yeah, secret is . . . better, huh? Right. Got it." She nodded a few times, seeming flustered.

• • •

I had fulfilled my mission as a time traveler.

But how could I get back to the future?

"I'll be back for you!"

That's what Akashi had told me, but it was unthinkable that she would come back here to pick me up. After the Coke Incident, the wake for the air conditioner would last all night. She couldn't show up in the time machine while people from the building were constantly coming and going.

In any case, I had to get out of the building. If yesterday-me showed up, there would be utter chaos.

"Ah, that bath really hit the spot," Ozu said as he waved a hand towel around. "Why did you come back early?"

"I had an errand to run."

"And you ran it?"

"Well, yeah. It wasn't that big of a deal."

"Meh-heh," replied Ozu with a sketchy smile.

Hanuki had sat down on the couch and was drinking straight from a plastic bottle of Coke. Higuchi had left room 210 open and was creeping around in its gloom. Akashi called to his back, "Master, the landlady was just calling for you!"

"Must be about the rent," Higuchi groaned.

Jogasaki was mopping up his sweat with a towel he had bought from the bathhouse custodian and grumbled, "It's so frigging hot," as he opened the door to room 209, as if it were the most natural thing in the world, and turned on the AC.

Hanuki set her Coke on the fridge and stretched. "So what are you guys gonna do now?"

"Master said we should have a wrap party," said Akashi. "And we can review the day's work."

"Oh, then I'll come with. Tell me how filming went."

Higuchi and Jogasaki started debating what to have for dinner.

"Are you going to come?" Akashi asked, but I shook my head.

"No, I have an errand to run."

I had to escape while I had the chance.

But as soon as I began walking down the hall, Ozu spread his arms and blocked my way. "Not so fast."

"What? Let me through."

"Why did you come back only to leave again right away?"

"Like I said, I have an errand to run."

"But didn't you tell me that you ran it already?"

"That was a different errand. I'm a busy guy."

"You've been acting really weird for a while now. You're keeping some kind of secret." He heaved an exaggerated sigh. "Why won't you be honest with me? Aren't we bosom buddies?"

"I don't recall ever giving you that sort of status."

"Cruel as always." He sulked before a grin appeared on his face. "So is it a woman?"

"H-h-hardly."

"This is you we're talking about, so there's no fooling me!"

He was so annoying I felt like I might lose my grip on reality. When I tried to shove him aside and leave, he tangled around me like a mollusk and pretended to cry. "You're so mean, you big meanie! I can't believe you would leave me for some woman you hardly even know!"

"Hey, I'm begging you, just let me go. If I don't leave now, there's going to be trouble!"

"Get a room, you two," Hanuki laughed.

After arguing for a bit, Ozu finally said, "Fine, whatever," and let go of me. "I'm no ogre, so if you want to go that badly, I'll let you. But it'll cost you. Yes, there's punishment."

"What do you want me to do?"

"Dance naked, duh."

"Why should I have to dance naked?"

"Because that's about the only thing that will heal the wounds you've inflicted on my heart! Where'd your bath bucket go? You can cover your privates with that for the traditional naked dance experience!"

I had to do whatever it would take to get out of this situation. I wrung every last bit of intelligence out of my brain. "Okay, I get it. I'll reveal my secret."

"Ooh," Ozu's interest was visibly piqued. "By all means, do tell us."

"Everyone go out to the laundry-drying area. Then you'll understand."

I waved everyone over with gestures that suggested the truth was at hand, inviting them to the laundry-drying area.

The sun had gone down, and the air was tinged with blue as if everything had sunk underwater.

Brushing a grimy sheet that had been hanging for ages aside, I leaned over the rusty railing and pointed at the landlady's yard. "What do you see there?"

The others approached the railing dubiously.

"It's the landlady's yard."

"Kecha's out there."

"Yes. And what is Kecha doing?"

"Looks like he's pouring the whole of his life force into digging a hole."

"Except that's not it. Look more closely."

Everyone was leaning over the railing peering out into the yard.

I quietly withdrew, swiftly ducked around the hanging sheet, and returned to the hallway.

No matter how much I wanted to escape the apartment building, yesterday-me would return at any moment. The

danger of running into him in the entryway was too great—
not that there was anywhere I could hide in the hallway. I
dove into room 209, climbed into the closet, and shut the door
from the inside. Buried among wrinkled clothes, cardboard
boxes, my porn library, and other random stuff, I held my
breath. I could hear everyone in the hallway looking for me.

You already know what happened next.

• • •

When I got back to Shimogamo Yusuiso, I heard animated
voices coming from the second floor.

"Where'd he go?" Ozu's voice was loudest of all.

Apparently, Higuchi and those guys were still hanging out
after our bath.

Upstairs, as I was walking down the hall, I saw that Higuchi
and Ozu were lurking at the other end. Jogasaki and Hanuki
were there, too. They were all peeking into the laundry-drying
area, opening doors, and shoving aside junk in the hallway,
looking for something. Just as I felt a worryingly cool breeze,
I noticed that the door to 209 was wide open. They were using
my air conditioner without asking again. Just as I was about
to raise my voice in anger, Akashi appeared from the laundry-
drying area. Apparently, while I was nursing my injured heart
on the Kamo River, she had returned from the used book fair.

"Oh!" she gasped when she saw me.

What's she so surprised for?

"What? Is something wrong?" I asked.

At the sound of Akashi's voice, Higuchi, Ozu, Jogasaki,

and Hanuki turned to look at me. They were all ah-ing or oh-ing in surprise. Their eyes were all on my bath bucket, and they contained a reverence I'd never felt before.

"Aha, I see. So you're all set, huh?" said Hanuki. "I'm in love."

Even Jogasaki's face said he thought better of me. "You really know how to get the party started."

Anyway, I snatched the remote out of Jogasaki's hand and turned off 209's air conditioner. "Don't just go using my AC whenever you feel like," I said as I set the remote on the mini fridge, where there was also a half-drunk bottle of Coke.

Akashi looked concerned.

"Are you really going to go through with it?"

"Go through with what?"

"With what? The, uh . . . thing . . ."

"All right, all right. Let's see that dance now!" Ozu grabbed my arm and stood me in the middle of the hallway. The others either sat on the couch or pulled up a stool and gazed at me with anticipation. Standing there speechless with my bath bucket, I looked around at them. What did they think I was going to do?

"Dance? What dance?"

"Oh, c'mon, we were just talking about it." Ozu smirked as he screamed, "A naked dance!"

"A naked dance? Why would I do that?"

"Oh, you're going to feign dignity now?" Higuchi said, stroking his chin.

Jogasaki frowned. "Hey, it's lame to stall. If you're gonna do it, be a man and do it."

"We won't take our eyes off you," said Hanuki.

"No, I just have no idea what you're talking about." When I looked to Akashi in desperation, she was hiding behind Higuchi. Her complex, subtle expression was a combination of embarrassment, resignation, and intellectual curiosity.

"You already have your prop, don't you?" Ozu pointed at my bath bucket. "You can just use that to dance—like this!" He held an invisible bath bucket over his nether regions and demonstrated.

I can remember the way Ozu was dancing with that wicked smirk on his face in minute detail even now. He was truly the personification of evil. And in truth, it was via this devilish dance that Ozu not only demolished my future, but also put the entire universe at risk of destruction.

Ozu's right arm bumped the fridge, and that was when the Coke bottle tipped over. The dark, frothy liquid poured out and rapidly spilled off the top of the fridge.

Akashi screamed, "The remote!"

I shoved Ozu out of the way and ran over, but it was too late.

Drenched in Coke, the remote lost all function.

• • •

That's how the Coke Incident of August 11 happened.

And yesterday-me had no way of knowing it, but that whole time, future-me was hiding in the closet of room 209.

"Ah, I see," I murmured to myself in the dark. "But now what do I do?"

THREE

August 12 Again

T he first time I ever spoke to Akashi was in February of this year.

That day, I had gone to the Masugata shopping street to pick up some things and was walking through the snow on my way home. Mount Hiei—visible from the Kamo Ohashi Bridge—the long bank of the Kamo River, and the pine trees on the Kamo River Delta were all white, as if they'd been coated in powdered sugar, and the quiet of the old capital sunk more deeply into my bones than usual.

I must have had a gloomy look on my face.

Late the previous fall, I'd been purged from the Keifuku Electric Railroad Research Society, and Ozu was the only one who came to visit me. Even Ozu popped by only while he was in the building visiting Seitaro Higuchi, who lived on the second floor. "I have a new little sister disciple," he said. Listening to his boasting, I would warm the tips of my fingers by the electric heater—that was the extent of my flavorless existence. The thought of returning to that freezing four-and-a-half-mat tatami room depressed me.

What kind of life am I going to live? Squinting my eyes to peer beyond the horizon, I still couldn't see the end of this utterly barren tatami galaxy.

On my way home, I stopped by the riding grounds of Tadasu no Mori on a whim.

The riding grounds, stretching north to south, were an expanse of snow. In August, the area would be crammed with tents for the used book fair, but now it was just a white void.

Standing there in the snow, I sighed.

It was so quiet, I could practically hear the snowflakes piling up as they fell.

Just then I noticed a woman walking ahead of me. She wore a red scarf and had a bag hung over her shoulder. I recognized her from behind; I had seen her around Shimogamo Yusuiso more than once.

As I was watching her, she tripped in the snow and fell.

Ah! I thought and rushed over, but she was up faster than I could get there. Then she calmly brushed the snow off her body and set off walking again, facing straight ahead.

My relief was only momentary, because ten seconds later she once again tripped spectacularly. I tried to run over to her again, but as before, my assistance was unnecessary. She was back on her feet and walking through the snow again in no time. She advanced through that silvery world like the very spirit of indomitability.

Looking down at my feet, I noticed a little bear plushie in the snow. It was a spongy gray bear with a bottom as soft and squishy as a newborn's.

"Hey!" I called ahead. "Did you drop a stuffed animal?"

When she stopped and turned around, she groped around her bag and made a surprised face.

I held up the bear and went through the snow to catch up to her. She took back the item she had dropped and said, "Thank you," in a white puff of breath. She was furiously kneading the bear with the serious look of a philosopher on her face.

"What is that?" I asked.

Her eyebrows instantly relaxed, and she smiled. "This is a mochiguma."

Apparently, she had five in different colors that she lovingly called the Fluffy Mochigumen Rangers. "Mochiguma" was a hard name to forget, but the smile on her face when she said "This is a mochiguma" was even more unforgettable.

• • •

August 12, six p.m.

It was about time for Akashi and the others to come back in the time machine.

I leaned against the wall in the hallway of Shimogamo Yusuiso facing Aijima, who was seated on the couch. While everyone had been abusing the time machine to hop between today and yesterday, Aijima alone stayed fixed in the present, watching all the drama with a chilly gaze.

Suspicion was plain in his voice as he asked, "So? What's the trick?"

Aijima stubbornly doubted the time machine's existence. In his eyes, the time machine was merely a kind of disappearing magic trick. The proof was that I, who had supposedly traveled to yesterday in the time machine, suddenly came out of room 209. Even though I explained that I had come back under my own steam, he wouldn't have it.

"Isn't it the same for everyone else, too?" he said. "Like they made it look like they disappeared, but really they're hiding somewhere around here?"

"Why would they go out of their way to do that?"

"That's what I'd like to know!" Aijima said indignantly. "Everyone's teamed up to tease me. It's seriously rude!"

If you're that skeptical, then why not try riding the thing for yourself?—I almost asked before swallowing the line. As someone who had just returned from a harrowing experience with time machine troubles, I didn't want to go out of my way to trigger another cosmic crisis. No one should be riding the time machine. There were too many risks; it was an absolutely impractical device.

"If you don't believe us, that's fine. Humanity isn't ready for time machines."

"So you admit that it's a trick?"

"Whatever floats your boat," I replied curtly, and Aijima fell silent.

It was a quiet evening; the only sounds were faint cicada cries. Suddenly the familiar flash filled the hallway, and a powerful whirlwind blew through. The time machine appeared before our eyes, and everyone riding on it collapsed in a heap.

Higuchi sluggishly got up and said, "Is everyone all right?"

"I'm good no matter what happens," said Ozu.

Hanuki said, "I mean, we're all right, but . . ." as she rubbed Akashi and Jogasaki's backs. The two who were susceptible to time machine sickness were both crouched on the floor. But Akashi was trying to crawl back to the time machine.

"I need to go back for him . . ."

"You don't need to go back for me, Akashi. I'm already here."

Everyone there turned to look at me and froze. They finally seemed to realize I was present. They all looked as if they were seeing a ghost.

"How did you get back?" asked Ozu.

I said, "I couldn't."

• • •

How did I return to today after being left behind in yesterday?

As I stated previously, after the Coke Incident, a wake for the air conditioner was held in room 209. Amid the echoes of the wooden fish Seitaro Higuchi struck, the residents of the building came one after the other to offer their condolences. There was a nonstop stream of people going through room 209, so I had no chance to escape the closet. Eventually, the rhythmic striking of the fish made me sleepy, and I started nodding off. Right about the time Higuchi said, "If you clear your mind, even a four-and-a-half-mat tatami room is as refreshing as Karuizawa—*katsu*!" was where my memory cut out.

When I woke up, there was light streaming through the crack of the closet door.

I was soaked with sweat and groggy, and it took me a little while to realize where I was.

Sitting there in a daze, I eventually heard some voices outside saying, "You little—!" and "I hardly felt that!" When I took a peek, I saw Ozu and myself exchanging rhythmic blows with hand towels. Apparently, I had drifted off in the closet and slept through the night.

Then Akashi said in a cool voice, "Oh, the idiocy of friendship."

As for what happened after that, you wise readers already know.

Tamura showed up, Higuchi woke up, Jogasaki and Hanuki showed up, the time machine was discovered, the meeting to discuss where to go with the time machine was held, the first exploratory squad (Higuchi, Hanuki, and Ozu) departed, Tamura showed up again, and the second exploratory squad (Akashi and I) departed.

I was hiding in the closet of room 209 that whole time.

I'm impressed I managed to hold out for twenty-four whole hours in that hellish heat, with nothing to eat or drink and unable to go to the bathroom. But most frustrating of all was being unable to prevent the follies of yesterday-us. If I had made so much as a peep, all my efforts would have come to naught. During Higuchi's crew's momentary return from yesterday, even while they ignored Jogasaki's warning and wrapped up the remote, I could do nothing but gnash my teeth, despite knowing that stupid move would only cause further tragedy.

I've never felt so liberated as I did when I could finally step out of the closet. To someone who has spent an entire day in a closet, a four-and-a-half-mat tatami room really is as refreshing as Karuizawa; the water that rushes from the tap is as cool and clear as the mountain streams of Kibune. I ecstatically stuck my head under the faucet to cool off, drank a barrelful of lukewarm barley tea, and was past ready for the bathroom, so I opened the door to the hallway.

Aijima was sitting on the couch by himself.

"What the heck?" His eyes went wide behind his glasses. "How long have you been in there?"

"Since yesterday! Forever!" I screamed in frustration as I ran to the toilet.

That was how I returned to August 12 under my own steam.

• • •

Hanuki was flabbergasted. "You spent the night in the closet? That's wild."

"Well, I didn't have any other options, you know?"

"Hmm?" She suddenly cocked her head. "She's going to go get you from yesterday, right? Which means there would be the you who is here and the you who came back. That makes two! What do we do about that?"

"That's why there's no need to go get me."

From yesterday evening until just a bit ago, there had been two of me. But one of me went to yesterday and would never come back. That is, the one who didn't come back stayed in the closet all night and became the one who was talking in the present.

But Hanuki wouldn't be satisfied so easily. "I feel like I'm being tricked somehow. Higuchi, does this make sense to you?"

"It doesn't make sense, but neither do I have a reason to complain."

Akashi stood and exhaled. Some of the color had returned to her cheeks. She walked slowly toward me and stared me down with her brow furrowed as if trying to ascertain my authenticity. "So I don't have to go get you?"

"I mean, I'm here, so . . ."

She sighed in relief. "I did mean to go back for you."

"I know. But you don't have to worry about it."

"So that's it, then?"

"Yep."

It was no wonder Akashi and the others had trouble accepting this abrupt end. Even I, who had spent a whole day coming back under my own steam, couldn't shake my doubt. *True, the flow of time has aligned. But is this really good enough?* Eventually, though, Higuchi solemnly declared, "All's well that ends well," and everyone experienced a bizarre sense of relief: *Well, it's probably fine.*

No one in particular turned to gaze at the time machine, and we all followed suit.

"Um." Tamura raised his hand. "Sorry to be so abrupt, but it's probably about time I took my leave."

"Oh, you're going back already?" said Ozu. "You should have some more fun before you go."

"Everyone seems pretty worried."

"'Everyone'?"

"When I went back to the future for the remote, the committee members, including me, gave me a stern talking-to. They said they were super worried because six months ago I was taking so long to come back. So it seems as though I should hurry home." Then he bowed politely. "Thank you all for your hospitality."

"Never come back." Jogasaki said angrily. "It was a real pain in the ass having you."

"Do you have to be so cold about it?" said Hanuki.

"Plus it's thanks to Tamura's quick wit that we have a remote for the AC," said Ozu. "I never would have thought of that. It was a truly ingenious idea."

"Don't pay attention to Jogasaki." Higuchi clapped Tamura on the shoulder. "Come visit anytime. Don't be a stranger."

"Thank you, Master. I appreciate you saying that."

When it came time to say goodbye, I found myself feeling surprisingly sad. It was like a cousin going home at the end of summer after coming over to play.

If Tamura hadn't come to the present day in the first place, we never would have plotted to retrieve yesterday's remote, and the universe wouldn't have been plunged into crisis. The utter lack of awareness as a time traveler on display in his words and deeds made me seethe with anger. But for some strange reason, I couldn't hate the guy. If we had been living in the same era, we probably would have been friends.

I could only hope that twenty-five years in the future, Tamura would avoid being misled by a weirdo like Seitaro Higuchi and would lead a meaningful student life.

"All right, everyone. Be well!" With that old-fashioned parting phrase, he pulled the lever, and the time machine vanished. His exit was as abrupt as his entrance.

The whole thing might as well have been a summer mirage.

"Guess he's home now." Akashi broke the silence.

In the emotional atmosphere, Aijima hesitantly spoke up. "So . . . it was actually a time machine?"

"You're just figuring that out?" Jogasaki replied in exasperation.

• • •

"Is Akashi there today?" The landlady's hoarse voice came over the speaker in the ceiling. "I'd like her to come pick up something she forgot."

Akashi looked up at the speaker in confusion. "I wonder what it is . . . I'll be right back."

While waiting for Akashi to come back, Higuchi and the guys started discussing what to do for the wrap party.

Really, the wrap party to celebrate finishing filming *Lives of Bakumatsu Weaklings* was supposed to have been held yesterday, but it was postponed due to the wake for the air conditioner.

They were getting all excited, saying, "We should make it an extra big deal since we just saved the universe." You wise readers already know that it was Akashi and I who saved the universe; everyone else did more harm than good, from start to finish. But I didn't have the energy to protest.

Hanuki pointed to a corner of the hallway and said, "Hey, isn't that Tamura's bag?"

Looking in the direction she was pointing, I saw a black shoulder bag. It was too dorky and un-futuristic to be anything else: it had to be Tamura's.

"For a time traveler, he sure is sloppy!"

"Maybe he'll come back for it."

"I'll hold onto it for now."

No matter how dorky it looked, it was a bag from the future. There was no telling what sort of space-time trouble might occur if it were left lying around.

I opened the door of room 209 and set Tamura's bag next to the sink.

Before closing the door, I glanced up at the air conditioner in my room.

Tamura had said that even a quarter century later, the same unit was still in operation in room 209. Having once been considered dead, this air conditioner had miraculously come back to life and would continue to be used for ages. That meant there had been no need to use the time machine in the first place. All we did was plunge the universe into crisis for no reason and then have a hell of time cleaning up after ourselves. It had been nothing other than a waste of a time machine.

As I was contemplating this ineffable shame, Ozu said, "You're treating me tonight, by the way."

"How does that work?"

"I mean, you were so cruel to me, saying I broke the remote. But the remote's gonna get fixed, so all your bullying was for nothing."

"But it's still a fact that you spilled the soda."

That was the moment a question appeared in my mind.

"Isn't there something weird about this?" I said.

"What's weird?"

"The remote that you spilled Coke on yesterday is the one

that Tamura brought from the future, right? And Akashi took it to the electrician today. So it'll get repaired and that will connect to the future?"

"Yeah, that's how the flow of time will align."

"But, no, how could that be possible? The flow doesn't align at all!"

I pulled an old blackboard out of the junk in the hallway and began drawing a visual aid showing the remote's movements across space-time.

Here's what I sketched out with the chalk:

Yesterday, Coke spills on the remote

→

The remote gets repaired

→

From then on, it continues to be used in room 209

→

Tamura brings it to yesterday from 25 years in the future

→

Coke spills on the remote

(Repeat)

"There is something a bit strange about this," murmured Higuchi, stroking his chin.

If this graphic was correct, then at some point the remote popped into existence out of nowhere and would travel in this twenty-five-year loop over and over forever.

That wasn't possible. Something had to be fundamentally wrong.

Just then, Akashi came walking down the hall. "Hey everybody, what's going on?"

"Akashi, we're in trouble."

"There's been a troublesome discovery on my end, too," she said, holding out a small, muddy object.

It was the thing the landlady had called over the speaker about, the thing Akashi had "forgotten." The landlady had found it in Kecha's doghouse. It didn't ring a bell, so it must have been something the kids filming the previous day left behind—that was her line of thought. But when Akashi took it in her hand, she had no doubt that it was something Kecha had dug up in the yard.

"Isn't this the AC remote?" she asked.

"No way," Jogasaki murmured. "The one I dropped in the swamp a hundred years ago?"

When we cleaned off the mud clinging to it, and cut off the tight plastic wrapping, a familiar-looking remote appeared. That is, the remote that had been dropped in the swamp ninety-nine years ago had spent those ninety-nine years underground before getting dug up by the passionate hole-digger Kecha.

As we were all speechless at this miraculous reunion spanning nearly a century, Hanuki said, "Maybe we can still use it."

"I doubt it. It's been almost a hundred years."

"But it looks fine."

"It *was* very tightly wrapped," Higuchi said, puffing his chest out with pride.

I put new batteries into the remote, aimed it at the air conditioner, and pushed the power button.

A beep sounded, and a cool breeze stroked my cheeks.

Everyone sighed in amazement.

"So that's how it happened?"

I overhauled my graphic on the blackboard:

The remote fell into a swamp 99 years ago

→

It spent 99 years in the ground

→

Kecha dug it up this morning

→

From then on, it continues to be used in room 209

→

Tamura brings it to yesterday from 25 years in the future

→

Coke spills on the remote

A truly epic journey across 124 years of time and space.

In that case, the absurdly abrupt ending where Ozu spills Coke on the remote really oozes a sense of fate.

"'The Remote That Leapt Through Time,'" said Akashi, a little embarrassed.

• • •

All's well that ends well. The only thing left was to party.

Seitaro Higuchi, who thought of himself as a man with an unparalleled love for fried rice, announced in a voice brimming with unshakable intention, "Midsummer fried rice is truly the dinner of youth!" Hanuki, who thought of herself as a woman with an unparalleled ability to drink beer like a fish, said, "Beer! Beer! Beer!" as if she were wishing on a shooting star.

So it was that our wrap party was to take place at a venue where fried rice and beer often met, a Chinese restaurant in Demachiyanagi.

When we left through the front door, I had the feeling I'd forgotten something.

"Aijima's glasses!"

While Jogasaki had been visiting ninety-nine years ago with the time machine, and we had all been looking for the remote, I had found the glasses, set them on my desk, and forgotten about them. "I'll go get them quick!" I said and took my shoes off to go back inside.

But as I was climbing the stairs, there was a loud noise on the second floor, and a strong wind blew down. I would recognize that sound anywhere. When I rushed up the stairs and peered down the hall, as I expected, a flustered Tamura was getting off the time machine.

"Hey, Tamura. Back already?"

"Oh, hello again," he said bashfully as he turned around. "I forgot my bag. Did you happen to see it?"

"No worries. I have it."

I opened the door to room 209. His bag was next to the sink where I'd left it.

When I grabbed it to hand to him, I accidentally dropped it. The impact knocked it open, and all sorts of little things, including a scroll-patterned hand towel, spilled onto the floor.

The moment I crouched down with a "Sorry!" my eyes latched onto a certain object. It was a dirty little bear plushie.

"Hey, Tamura. What's that?"

"This is a mochiguma." He explained as he packed up his things. "When I moved out to live on my own, my mom made me take it. 'Life in a four-and-a-half-mat tatami room is lonely, so take this with you,' she said. I don't really need it, of course, but, you know. She has a bunch more and calls them the Fluffy Mochigumen Rangers . . ."

No matter how marked by the years it was, I could never mistake the curve of that soft, squishy bottom.

I vividly recalled the snow-covered riding grounds. Snowflakes fluttering down, Akashi's footprints, the bear plushie in the snow. Why would Tamura, from twenty-five years in the future, have this? There could only be one answer.

"Are you Akashi's kid?"

"Hmm. Well, it would seem that way." He closed his bag and stuck his tongue out.

"Why didn't you say anything?!"

"How could I say something like that to her face?" He smiled warmly. "Even I have some awareness as a time traveler. I understand that if history changes in some weird way, I'd have problems. Tamura isn't even my real name. My dad was adopted into the family, so my name is actually Akashi."

"Holy wow."

"Please don't tell Mom. She still doesn't know anything."

"That's fine," I groaned. "But that means you knew everything? Everything that would happen up to now? Did you hear from your mom—I mean, Akashi?"

"No, it's not like that," Tamura said as he boarded the time machine. "She never tells me about her student days because it embarrasses her, and Dad has barely told me anything about how they met . . . He's always like, 'There's nothing so worthless to speak of as a love mature.' So I only know bits and pieces. If he had told me more, maybe I would have been able to play my cards better . . . But still, we averted the cosmic crisis and saved the air conditioner, so I have no complaints. All's well that ends well!

"This time it's really goodbye," Tamura said as he dialed in his destination. "My friends twenty-five years from now are waiting for me. We're going to go to the Chinese place in Demachiyanagi to celebrate our successful time travel."

"Wait a second!" I ran over to the time machine in a panic. "Just tell me one thing. Who's your dad?"

Tamura wagged a finger and clicked his tongue like a character in an American movie. "Ah-ah-ah. I can't do that. If I told you, the future could change. Why would I take such a risk? There's my responsibility as a time traveler to consider." Then he smirked. "You need to seize the future on your own."

"You talk awfully pretty for such a dork."

"That is one thing about me." He squeezed one eye closed. It was so awkward, I couldn't tell what he was doing, but after the fact, I realized it must have been a wink.

"I wish you luck! Now, farewell!" With those old-fashioned parting words, Tamura once again returned to the future.

After standing there dazed for a moment, I grabbed Aijima's glasses case and went back. When I reached the entrance, everyone was sick of waiting for me. They shouted, "You took forever!" I figured I should keep the conversation I had with Tamura to myself. When I handed the case over to Aijima, he was thrilled. "Yes, those! Those are the ones!"

Akashi was the only one who seemed to suspect anything. As we set off down the gravel path outside the door, she asked, "Did something happen?"

"No." I shook my head. "It was nothing."

• • •

We wandered out of Shimogamo Yusuiso into Shimogamo Izumikawacho.

Thanks to the time machine, it felt as if I'd been trapped in yesterday and today for ages. And in reality, I'd lived an extra twenty-four hours compared with the others, since I had been stuck in the closet. Of course these two days would feel terribly long.

The sight of street corners sunken in indigo darkness, the coolness of the occasional evening breeze—it felt like it had been an awfully long time since I had tasted either.

"I can't believe it. I really can't believe it." Aijima muttered as he walked along. "Just going between yesterday and today is such a waste of a time machine. There were so many more significant ways you could have used it. You could have at least brought back something of historical value."

I understood how he felt, but I didn't want to hear that from him.

When I said, "We solved the mystery of the kappa legend," Jogasaki snapped at Higuchi as if he had just remembered.

"I haven't forgiven you, you know."

"You don't give up, do you? You became a historical figure!" Higuchi laughed at the night sky.

"But we're sure lucky the AC got fixed, Master. For a moment there I really wondered how we'd cope."

"Mm. Now we'll be able to survive the lingering heat."

Listening to Higuchi and Ozu's exchange, I found myself interrupting: "What are you guys talking about? Please don't spend all your time in my room."

"No, no, we don't even need to."

"What do you mean?"

"The chilled air from your room filters into mine."

According to Higuchi, the thin walls of Shimogamo Yusuiso had gaps all over the place. Apparently, Higuchi had been able to spend each summer in comfort thanks to the cool air leaking from room 209. Then the previous occupant, a legal student who had been studying for his next attempt at the bar exam, left. That was when I, who lived downstairs, was chosen for the move.

Come to think of it, Ozu was the one who let me know the room was empty; it was Ozu who made impassioned arguments to convince me to move; and it was Ozu who helped me carry all my stuff upstairs. What a dope I was for thinking he was just trying to atone for us getting driven out of the Keifuku Electric Railroad Research Society.

"Ohhh, so that's how it works," said Hanuki. "I always wondered why that room was so chilly."

I was speechless. "My good sir," said Higuchi in a friendly tone. "I'll approve your disciplehood. I hope you'll stay with me for many years to come."

Akashi turned around with a smile. "Hey, good for you."

But all I could do was smile vaguely.

Is this really a good thing? Am I not just being preyed on by an evil bunch? Have I not just stepped down the path to ruin?

Ozu sidled up to me and put his arm around my shoulder.

"Since that's how it is, I'm looking forward to being disciples together, brother."

"Are you only capable of sinister plots?"

Ozu put on his usual yokai grin and laughed his head off.

"It's my love language."

"Gross—you can spare me," I replied.

• • •

When we made it through the pine trees, the clear, indigo sky opened up beautifully overhead.

We all went down the riverbank to the end of the Kamo River Delta. The sound of the water swelled. Seitaro Higuchi stood firmly at the delta's tip, like a captain at the bow of his ship. The Takano River coming from the northeast and the Kamo River coming from the northwest mingled before our eyes to continue flowing south as one Kamo River.

In the lights reflecting here and there, the surface of the water looked like a sheet of metallic paper being waved like a stage prop. Before my eyes lay Kamo Ohashi. The lamps in a well-mannered row along the bridge's railing cast an orangey glow, and shining cars crisscrossed without end. Along the Kamo riverside sinking into darkness, there were

people walking their dogs and students out enjoying the evening cool.

Once I had crossed the stepping stones to the west side of
the Kamo River, Akashi alone caught up to me.

"They won't just walk, huh?"

"Do they even want to have a wrap party? I'm starving to
death over here."

Eager for fried rice and beer, I turned around to look at the
delta.

Seitaro Higuchi was standing at the point with his arms
held out, surrounded at a distance by the other people in the
area; Ozu had gotten the cuffs of his pants wet accidentally
stepping into the river, and Hanuki was pointing at him and
laughing. Jogasaki spread his arms and hovered to make sure
she didn't fall in. Aijima stood alone, polishing his glasses
as he smirked to himself about some funny memory. What a
bunch of weirdos.

Why am I with these people? I wondered.

Yet the whole scene was strangely nostalgic. I couldn't
help but feel that I'd been present for a similar moment in the
past. It was this intense feeling that everything was repeating
itself—genuine déjà vu this time, I suppose.

Mount Daimonji was visible beyond the streetscape across
the river.

"There's something that's been on my mind for a while
now," Akashi said, standing next to me. "Even with a time
machine, I don't think you can change the past."

I told her that couldn't be true. "The reason the past
didn't change is that you and me aligned the flow of time.

Otherwise Higuchi and Ozu would have just done whatever they felt like . . ."

"But in the end, that's what everyone did, isn't it?"

Now that she mentioned it, yeah, that was true. Hanuki had boldly mingled with past us to watch the filming, and Higuchi even stole the Vidal Sassoon from his yesterday self. Yet the flow of time miraculously aligned. You could even say it aligned a little too well.

But if using the time machine wouldn't change the past, then what was all our hard work for?

"I tried thinking of time as a book," Akashi said as she looked up into the sky. "The reason it seems to flow from past to future is that that's the only way we can experience it. For example, if there were a book here, we wouldn't be able to grasp all its content at once. All we can do is turn the pages and read them one at a time. But the content itself is already inside the book. The distant past and the distant future are both . . ."

I finally understood what she was getting at.

"You mean everything was already decided."

"If a time machine appears in the future, that detail would obviously be written in the book. Which means that everything caused by the time machine would also be in the book. So maybe 'You can't change the past' isn't the best way to put it. More like, everything has already happened. It's not an issue of changing it or not."

"That makes it sound like we have no freedom in the future."

"But we have no idea what'll happen in the future. If we

know nothing, we can do anything. Maybe that's what freedom means."

"Well, we know Tamura will be born, at least."

"True," Akashi laughed. "He was so interesting. I already
kind of miss him."

Then she gazed at the Kamo River for a little while, mull-
ing something over.

When I asked her what she was angsting about, she answered that going by her thought process just now, she would
have to change the end of *Lives of Bakumatsu Weaklings*.

Right, the movie was about the Meiji Restoration being
disrupted as the result of protagonist Susumu Ginga time-
slipping into the Bakumatsu period. According to what
Akashi was saying just now, it would have to be a story
about how the Meiji Restoration was unavoidable, no matter
what kind of outrage Susumu Ginga perpetrated during his
time slip. When I asked, "You're not going to retake it, are
you?" she laughed.

"Ha, no. It is what it is. I want to film something new."

"Yeah, I think that's a better idea."

"I want to do that story you were mentioning about the guy
wandering through four-and-a-half-mat tatami rooms," she
said. "I think it's a great idea."

Just then, the perfect title came to me, like a divine revelation.

"How about calling it *The Tatami Galaxy*?"

"Nice," she said, her face lighting up.

There was one other idea that seemed ready to film. All
the hijinks that ensued with Tamura and the time machine
between today and yesterday at Shimogamo Yusuiso would

make a great movie. She could simply film it at Shimogamo Yusuiso; the cast, except for Tamura, were right there.

"What to call it, though?"

"I've already decided."

"Oh yeah?"

"*Summer Time Machine Blues.*" She smiled. "Good, right?"

• • •

The Tatami Galaxy and *Summer Time Machine Blues* . . .

I was pleased to be able to continue assisting Akashi with her film projects. We were firm in our intention to bring these lovable, trashy flicks to fruition and drive the club boss Jogasaki up the wall.

But the most pressing issue was the Gozan Okuribi.

The evening of the previous day, August 11, I had invited Akashi to watch the ritual fires, and she had agreed to go with me.

But I only did it because today-Akashi told me to invite yesterday-Akashi. I could hardly imagine that an invitation so devoid of initiative would remain valid between a man and a woman. Yet to Akashi on August 11, it appeared that I had invited her on my own initiative. Given that she had accepted under those circumstances, it was probably safe to infer that she didn't hate me. But Akashi already knew that the one who invited her was August 12-me, and that I did so following the directions of her August 12-self. Thus, there was no way that current Akashi would take yesterday's promise seriously. Frankly, the whole thing was too confusing.

When I looked to the delta, Ozu and the others were finally walking our way.

"C'mon, everybody, let's hurry up and get this party going!" she shouted to them with a big wave.

Staring at her profile, I recalled what Tamura had said.

His parents had met as university students. If his mom was Akashi, then who in the world was his dad? Someone I was well-acquainted with? Some complete unknown?

How should I know?! is what I really wanted to say.

A huge chain of identical four-and-a-half-mat tatami rooms continuing beyond time and space . . . It felt like yesterday was the same as today, and tomorrow and today would also be the same; I wanted to bid farewell to this fruitless cycle as of right now. I took a deep breath to get ready to talk to Akashi.

That was when she whispered. "Oh hey, where are we gonna watch the Gozan Okuribi from?"

• • •

I don't think I'll ever forget that summer evening.

So it was that our summer proceeded toward its end. It would never be repeated, and even if we used a time machine, we could never get it back.

How my relationship with Akashi developed after that is a deviation from the point of this manuscript. Therefore, I shall refrain from writing the charming, bashfully giddy details. You probably don't want to pour your time down the drain reading such detestable drivel, anyhow. There's nothing so worthless to speak of as a love mature.

Afterword

by Makoto Ueda (playwright, director)

After the myth of spring comes the myth of summer.

It's the summer myth of rotten university students who go out of their way in the humidity and the clamor of cicadas to gather in an apartment like a topographical pocket of hot air to film a movie that need not have been filmed at all and end up breaking the air conditioner remote.

As if it's not already sweltering, a time machine complicates things, and the threads of fate tangle, growing as warm as an outlet overloaded with cords. The story progressively heats up, cramped with one foot in yesterday and one in today, sweating stickily in the face of cosmic collapse, following Ozu who is following the protagonist who is following Akashi, and the remote straddles a hundred years. Once the threads all connect, as if the race has been rigged, a date invitation originating who-knows-where gives Akashi and the protagonist a sudden prod in the back with an invisible hand.

Broiling, uncomfortably warm, it's that kind of conveniently plotted myth. The Kamo River is cool in the evening with a breeze of divine breath.

The spring myth—the book that came before this one—is *The Tatami Galaxy*.

It's a myth in which the protagonist, in pursuit of a rose-colored campus life as the cherry blossoms flutter, chooses his university club and gets two years of his life ruined—repeatedly—by his undesirable pal, the loathsome Ozu.

It was written fifteen years before the summer myth. The ecology of these Kyoto-dwelling rotten university students is depicted with a raw familiarity, and apparently has its roots in author Morimi's own student days.

As someone rotting at a university in Kyoto at that time, a sympathy I couldn't help but feel upon reading it tickled me till I writhed, which led to me getting to write the screenplay for the 2010 anime adaptation.

That was our first official collaboration, and since then I've written the screenplays for *The Night Is Short, Walk on Girl* and *Penguin Highway*, as well as written and directed the stage adaptation of *The Night Is Short, Walk on Girl*—each time finding myself at the mercy of Morimi's racing, romping pen as I somehow manage to retell his work in script form.

Arriving at wit's end faced with Morimi's uninhibited style is fun for me—you could even say it's the joy of my life—and as I was thinking, rather like a loathsome, undesirable pal, that if I could become his personal screenwriter I could live out the rest of my days in peace (*Allow me to accompany you!*), Morimi came to bounce something surprising off of me.

On the occasion of writing a sequel to the spring myth, he wanted to use my play *Summer Time Machine Blues* as the basis and have the Tatami crew go wild within that plot structure. It was an unusual plan, a devilish idea. I was honored, and in the same moment a thrill ran through me. An independent derivative work. An outrageous conversion that might or might not even work. I wondered for a moment if the author would be upset, but it was the author himself proposing the idea.

Summer Time Machine Blues is one of the flagship productions of my theater company, Europe Kikaku, and was first performed in Kyoto during the summer of 2001. It was a life-size projection of our still–university student days in our theater club box.

In the room where rotten university students hang out as a science fiction club in name only, a time machine shows up one summer, and together with the photography club kids from the room over, they go on a little time trip to the previous day to retrieve the air conditioner's remote before it breaks. That eventually causes logical paradoxes, and in order to make everything consistent, the members run between campus and the bathhouse, yesterday and today. Unskilled baseball, Vidal Sassoon, a pharmacy mascot, love, and movies. These were the colorful little things that surrounded us.

As a fan of time travel stories myself, what I think really makes *Summer Time Machine Blues* so fun is the fact that it's an *ensemble* piece.

Novels, movies, and so on generally depict time machine stories from the perspective of a single person. When the protagonist pulls the lever, the space-time before them warps, and the past or future appears. The camera follows the protagonist, and the time trip progresses as a first-person adventure.

For the stage, I put a twist on this so that multiple characters would ride the time machine and the camera wouldn't follow them on each trip; I aimed for a time machine story from an objective perspective. The idea was to peek into this room where the time machine appeared as if into an aquarium. Or like if there were a Drifters skit based around a time machine. The plan went well, and with the busy coming and goings of the rabble and the increasing number of time trips on a machine that keeps appearing and disappearing, it ended up a frenetic sci-fi ensemble comedy.

Morimi said he wanted to keep that lively impression, but do it with the strong personalities of the Tatami characters and that first-person narration.

"When you make it a novel, it's hard to get the frenetic atmosphere across," Morimi whimpered to me any number of times while he was writing. I mused, *Maybe novels and theater really are different beasts?* and felt sort of bad in a *Sorry . . .* kind of way, while also thinking, *This was your idea*, but there wasn't really anything I could do to help, so I simply looked forward to the finished manuscript.

Keeping Morimi's struggles in mind—apparently there weren't enough characters, so he had to keep the already tight plot going with a limited ensemble—the thought that, "Those characters are, at this very moment, dancing in the service of that incredible pain-in-the-butt of a plot" gave me butterflies, irresponsible though that may have been. It was the exact opposite of my labors as a screenwriter.

Thus, *The Tatami Time Machine Blues*, this summer myth written on a bubbling boil like a forbidden experiment, was filled with the excessive calories of youth reduced down, as well as the cooling presence of the divine.

I do have the sense that this is a story I came up with, but there's no question that this is Morimi's book, a new chapter in the nostalgic yet novel Tatami mythology.

The fever and cacophony are even more tremendous than in the stage version; the futility of *Lives of Bakumatsu Weaklings* is beyond words, the dusky presence of the cosmos so chilling; I want to join the wrap party at the Chinese joint; action, thrills, yes, but the entirely unnecessary rambling about the Keifuku Electric Railroad Research Society made me so happy, like, "This! This is the stuff!"

In particular, for the interactions between the protagonist and Akashi, the ink of emotions seemed to seep ceaselessly from Morimi's pen, and after being made to feel something indecent at the end of that progression and then getting dismissed with that final line, I remain in that summer. When Morimi rewrites a play as a novel, this kind of giant emotional youth fantasy picture scroll is born.

Well, I'm not sure if this can really be called an afterword or not, but this whole experience was more than I could have hoped for.

The brash characters I once loved live anew in a somewhat nostalgic story—a profoundly mysterious summer myth experience.

Multiple threads of fate tangled and I wrote the screenplay for *The Tatami Time Machine Blues* anime, and now

I'm writing the afterword for the paperback edition of the novel. Maybe Morimi will write the story of a refined playwright trapped in what Manabu Makime calls our "perpetual fiction machine." Please let me write the screenplay if you do.

A Note from the Translator

English readers are so lucky! You get the sequel less than a year after the original. In Japan, *The Tatami Galaxy* was published in 2004, and *Tatami Time Machine Blues* was announced about a month ahead of its publication in 2020. It was a complete shock to get a sequel sixteen years after the fact (not the least of which because Morimi fans have been patiently waiting for the end of the *Uchōten kazoku* [*Eccentric Family* is the anime title in English] trilogy. Zero shade, of course; we will wait till the end of time if necessary). And what a strange concept for one—based on a play-which-is-also-a-movie by Makoto Ueda? I'm a huge Morimi fan, so I was thrilled, but also nervous. How was this going to work? I officially apologize here for ever doubting him.

Summer Time Machine Blues is a great play/movie on its own, much like, say, *A Christmas Carol*. But just as the Muppets managed to do a beloved version of the latter, Morimi knocked the former out of the park with his gang of rotten university students, as you just read. Every part that deviates from the original does so in the most *Tatami Galaxy*–like way. All the nods to or outright quotes from the first book are so satisfying—not that you even need to have read that one to enjoy this one.

There are some other things you needn't have read to enjoy this book. For example: *Romance of the Three Kingdoms.* "Meet a boy after one summer, and you'll hardly recognize him!" is a riff on a quote from there that goes something more like, "If you haven't seen a boy in three days, take a good look at him" in the original; the meaning being that he'll have grown and changed over the course of that time. Naturally, after a whole summer of the self-improvement the protagonist dreams of, he would be unrecognizable. There are also references to a poem by Du Fu, a quote from Saneatsu Mushanokōji, *The Art of War*, and a handful of other sources for the geekiest readers (in both languages) to pick up on.

Rendering period speech can be a challenge in any language, but for the chaotic scene near the beginning of this book it was simple to arrive at the choice of transliterating instead of translating the Japanese, because the characters themselves are clearly just shouting random archaic words. They're more like a gaggle of honking geese than a group of actors at that point. For the record, *gowasu* is a polite form of "be" and *ojaru* is a respectful form of "go"/"come"/"be" (for a living thing).

Some might argue that there's nothing so worthless to speak of as a translation well-executed. To them, I'm supposed to be invisible, so what's all this translator's note drivel? *If you have to explain the charming, bashfully giddy details, did you even do your job right?* Here's to hoping my note wasn't too detestable.

—Emily Balistrieri

Here ends Tomihiko Morimi's
The Tatami Time Machine Blues.

The first edition of this book was printed
and bound at Lakeside Book Company
in Harrisonburg, Virginia, October 2023.

A NOTE ON THE TYPE

The text of this novel was set in Sabon, an old-style serif typeface created by Jan Tschichold between 1964 and 1967. Drawing inspiration from the elegant and highly legible designs of the famed sixteenth-century Parisian typographer and publisher Claude Garamond, the font's name honors Jacques Sabon, one of Garamond's close collaborators. Sabon has remained a popular typeface in print, and it is admired for its smooth and tidy appearance.

HarperVia

An imprint dedicated to publishing international voices,
offering readers a chance to encounter other lives and other
points of view via the language of the imagination.